THREE HOLIDAY TALES IN ONE!

SUSAN KIERNAN-LEWIS

SAN MARCO PRESS

INTRODUCTION

Get ready for the holidays with two different American expats as they manage to celebrate Thanksgiving and Christmas in France in three different novellas.

A Thanksgiving in Provence is a snapshot view of the trickier elements of pulling together a turkey dinner in a small French village—compounded by a theft that has family and friends pointing the finger at each other.

A Provençal Christmas brings all the color and emotion of celebrating Christmas in a provincial French village—with a strong *Gift of the Magi* twist you won't see coming.

A French Country Christmas gives a light-hearted taste of the season in the middle of the apocalypse. Can't imagine it? That's what the people of the French village of Chabanel said too before it happened to them!

All three holiday tales are clean reads with no sex, violence, murders or explicit language—but plenty of adorable dogs and a few clever cats.

Both *A Thanksgiving in Provence* and *A Provençal Christmas* include holiday recipes to make your holidays that much brighter.

THE FIRST WEEK OF ADVENT

Maggie looked at the array of small toys and trinkets on the dining room table. A plastic fighter jet. A ballerina that fit over a child's index finger to make it dance. A small bag of colored marbles. There were more things for Jemmy than for Mila. Would she notice? Would she care? Will there be tears?

"Can you just explain to me why we have to do Christmas morning less than a week after Thanksgiving?" she asked her husband who stood in their kitchen in front of the new Cornue stove—an early Christmas present to himself.

"You know why," Laurent said as he reached for the Herbes de Provence and sprinkled it liberally over the bubbling stew in the pot he was stirring on the stove.

"Well, it makes no sense." Maggie blew an errant strand of hair from her face as she taped down the ends of a gaily colored package on the table before her. "It flies in the face of serenity and peace and all that other crap you're supposed to feel at Christmas when you have to run around and create Christmas morning before Thanksgiving is even over."

Laurent turned and smiled at her.

Which just made her madder.

"I really don't have time for this," Maggie said. "My blog post was supposed to have gone out yesterday and I don't even have an idea of what I'm writing about! Danielle and Jeannette Pernon drove over this morning with about a dozen almond tarts and I know they were looking around like they were wondering where *their presents* were."

"I'm sure they had no such expectation, *chérie*," Laurent said. "Besides, it is just how it is done here. As you well know."

The hell of it was, he was right. It was just an unfortunate coincidence that one of the days the French celebrated Christmas—at least the gift-giving part—was December fifth when most Americans had barely succeeded in pushing back from their Thanksgiving dinner tables.

The fact that Maggie and Laurent's two children Mila and Jemmy fully expected presents —as all children throughout France did—six days after Thanksgiving made the bad timing irrelevant.

"At least we only have to fill their shoes," Maggie said with a sigh.

"Think of it as a token," Laurent said. "To tide them over."

"Yeah, tell that to Jemmy."

Their oldest boy Jemmy was six years old and well aware of the details and implied contract of December fifth as well as Christmas in general. As for their youngest, Mila was just catching on but Maggie had no doubt Jemmy would bring her up to speed quickly enough.

"Last year Jemmy put out *your* shoes instead of his own,"

Maggie reminded her husband. "I can't believe you let him get away with that."

Laurent laughed and then tasted the stew before putting the wooden spoon down and turning to Maggie. He took her into his arms and looked into her eyes.

Maggie knew very well what he was doing. He typically did it when he wanted to disarm her or defuse a situation. Damn him, it always worked too.

"What is really bothering you?" Laurent asked in his thick French accent.

This close, he smelled like cinnamon and garlic. A very odd but somehow heavenly combination, Maggie thought. That and his uncanny ability to read her mind tended to make her melt in his arms.

"Is it because we didn't go home to Atlanta this year?"

Maggie shook her head. It was true she missed not seeing her parents at Christmas, and when her mother told her about their cruise to Mexico, it made Maggie wonder if she were the only one in the family who still cared about traditions and reunions. It was frankly unnerving.

Had the baton been passed down to her? Already?

The insistent aroma of cinnamon and pine needles permeated the air around her as Maggie glanced at the table full of trinkets, little toys, and wrapping paper and realized that her mother had done all of these things—felt all of these things—in her time. And now, instead of threading popcorn on a string or positioning candles in the windows of their Buckhead mansion to beckon home the children she adored, she'd announced that she'd rather slap on sunscreen and have waiters bring her beachside mojitos.

Maggie shook her head as if to clear it. While it was true *she* was right in the thick of trying to create happy holiday memories for her own family, she couldn't imagine wanting to be shed of it all, or of preferring a beach vacation to experiencing the joy of the season.

Except the joy of the season has to do with family, she thought. And Elspeth and John's family were a long way from Atlanta, Georgia these days.

"*Chérie?*"

She gave Laurent's arm a squeeze.

"No. I guess it's because I don't understand why Mom and Dad didn't want to come to France instead of going to the beach. It's like they've given up on Christmas."

"It is very cold here," Laurent said. "It is possible to imagine why they would prefer to be elsewhere."

"Their family is here."

"Ah. It is the argument for which there is never a right answer," Laurent said. He released her and turned back to his kitchen. Maggie knew Laurent had issues with his own family. In her mind it was nothing short of a miracle that he was able to be the amazing father and husband that he was, considering he had absolutely no template to work with.

It also explained why he thought nothing of Maggie's parents ditching Christmas with family when they could lie on the beach instead.

"*Maman! Maman!*"

Maggie quickly threw a tablecloth over the top of the unwrapped presents and turned to see Mila and Jemmy coming from the stairs. Jemmy was dressed for the day but Mila still wore her pajamas. She clutched a battered stuffed lamb in her arm.

"Are those ours?" Jemmy asked excitedly, his eyes wide and focused on the dining room table.

"Never mind that," Maggie said sternly, but with a smile. "Your papa has your breakfast ready."

Jemmy ran to the kitchen and hopped up on one of the

kitchen stools across from the breakfast bar and Laurent slid a plate of scrambled eggs toward him.

Mila stopped in front of Maggie and smiled up at her mother.

"*Moi, j'adore* Christmas," she said dreamily. "Lambie does too. It's the bestest time of the year."

Maggie felt her heart swell with love as she watched her youngest join her brother at the breakfast bar where Laurent poured small jugs of milk for them.

Had her mother felt like this once upon a time too? she wondered. Had Elspeth regarded her husband and her own two children once and felt so happy and so full of love for her dear ones that it was simply impossible to imagine that life would one day be empty and dull?

Dinner that night was Laurent's usual masterpiece.

Too cold for dining al fresco—always Laurent's preference—he had staged the dining room using their best linens and china. The silver flatware and crystal wine glasses reflected the candlelight and the fairy lights that Jemmy and Maggie had hung from the chandelier over the table.

When Mila came into the room—dressed in her satin party dress with its crinoline petticoats—she clapped her hands together in awe.

This is what Christmas is about, Maggie thought as she watched her children gaze at the lights, the glitz, the tinsel, and the mysterious packages under the towering fir tree Laurent had cut in the forest and brought in the morning before. Just the tree seemed to fill the entire house with wonder and delight, looming majestically and anchoring the room where before there had been only a simple brass *torchiere* lamp.

The wonder of this time of year is in the air, in the aromas that surround us, and in the laughter of loved ones, near and dear to us.

The doorbell rang and Jemmy and Mila both squealed, setting off their little dog, Petit-Four who began barking. The two children and the dog raced to the front door to let in their first guests.

Because most years they had always gone home to Atlanta for Christmas, Maggie and Laurent had missed the traditional December festival of friends and neighbors, feasting and gifting. When she saw the effort Laurent had gone to—not just on tonight's dinner but the preparation for the *réveillon* next week—she realized how important this time of the year was to him and how much he had given up when he went with her to Atlanta instead.

Maggie made a silent vow that they would celebrate Christmas in St-Buvard from now on. This was home now. While her mother had hinted that if Maggie and the children would come home to Atlanta for Christmas, she and her father would of course stay and do Christmas as usual, Maggie couldn't help think that her mother had been relieved not to host them.

I'm not there yet, Maggie thought as she listened to her children's laughter and excited voices. *And God willing, I never will be.*

She grinned as Danielle and Jean-Luc Alexandre entered the large stone foyer of Domaine St-Buvard, Maggie and Laurent's large nineteenth century *mas*. Although the place had been a wreck when Laurent inherited it nine years ago from his bachelor uncle, they had worked hard to renovate it.

Laurent's sizable inheritance from his aunt last spring had helped too.

"*Joyeux Noël*, Maggie!" Jean-Luc bellowed as he entered the hall with little Mila in his arms. Jemmy was holding Danielle's heavy winter coat and his eyes danced with anticipation.

"*Joyeux Noël*, Jean-Luc," Maggie said. She quickly kissed the old gentleman on both cheeks before embracing his wife. The couple was in their late sixties and owned the vineyard that bordered Maggie's and Laurent's property. In spite of the age difference they were Maggie and Laurent's closest friends.

"Oh, something smells wonderful! Can I help?" Danielle said as she headed for the kitchen.

Laurent met her at the kitchen door and they embraced. "*Joyeux Noël*, Danielle and Jean-Luc. Drinks, yes?" He ushered them to the antique mahogany buffet where there was a tray of champagne flutes.

"Oh! The dining room is beautiful!" Danielle said. "So festive!"

"Me and Mama did that," Jemmy said. "I climbed on a ladder to get the ones up high."

"*C'est magnifique*, Jemmy," Jean-Luc said, ruffling the boy's hair. "Truly *superbe*."

Laurent poured four Kir Royales. What with the burning of the entire grape harvest, it had been a hard year for all of them. But they had come out on the other side together.

"Is it time to talk about 2017 yet?" Jean-Luc said with a grin.

"Jean-Luc!" Danielle said. "Let us say goodbye to 2016 first."

Laurent poured a tiny glass of champagne and *crème de cassis* and handed it to Jemmy.

"Laurent..." Maggie said with a frown.

Laurent topped up the child's glass with *gazeuse limonade* and poured another glass of only lemonade for Mila.

"Everyone must have something to toast with," Laurent said as he held up his glass and everyone followed.

"We are together and all is well. *Salut, mes amis* and *Joyeux Noël!*"

"*Joyeux Noël!*"

After the first sip Jemmy made a face and eyed Mila's drink enviously.

"To friends and to the happiest of Christmases," Danielle said as she raised her glass.

"Here here," Maggie said as she felt the warmth of the moment envelope her in a penumbra of happiness.

A few minutes later the rest of the guests arrived—mostly friends of Laurent from the village. By the time Mila and Jemmy were ready to set out their shoes for Pere Noël and go to bed, Laurent was fully into the role of host, topping up people's drinks while making sure the *gougeres* didn't burn and his mustard and white wine braised chicken would be ready to go when it was time. Jean-Luc kissed both children and went to help Laurent.

Maggie couldn't help notice how being a provisional grandfather to her children had given the older man a special *joie de vivre* that he'd never had before. Especially at Christmastime when he got to play Pere Noël for them on Christmas Day.

Danielle took Jemmy's hand as Maggie took Mila's and they led the children upstairs. Maggie noticed that Danielle was carrying a large envelope.

"I found something old in my attic this afternoon," Danielle said as they mounted the steps.

"Oh?" Maggie asked, feeling the warmth of the two champagne cocktails she'd downed a little too quickly.

"Something I thought Monsieur Jemmy and Mademoiselle Mila might like."

As they reached the top of the stairs Danielle opened the envelope and pulled out what looked at first like a large square of cardboard.

But in the dim light of the hall sconces, Maggie could see it was an Advent calendar—a very old one.

"It's beautiful, Danielle," Maggie said. "Whose was it?"

"It was in the attic so it might have been Jean-Luc's mother's or perhaps his niece's."

At the mention of Madame Renoir, Maggie felt a flinch of sadness. She had heard just before Thanksgiving that Madame Renoir had passed away in the sanatorium where she'd gone to live nine years ago. Maggie had wanted to visit, but had been warned that seeing Maggie again could be very unpleasant for the older woman. And nobody, least of all Maggie, had thought it was worth the risk to find out.

"What's a Advent calendar?" Jemmy asked as he took the calendar from Danielle. He flicked open one of the tiny windows.

"It's a way of getting ready for Christmas," Maggie said. "You open up a little window for each day of Advent leading up to Christmas Day."

"What for?" he asked.

"Well, because in a lot of ways the wait is nearly as important as the actual day," Maggie said. "It helps us get ready." She looked at Danielle who smiled and nodded.

"For the day baby Jesus is born," Mia said softly.

"That's right, darling."

"*Merci, Mamere*," Jemmy said to Danielle. He had clearly lost interest and handed the calendar to Mila.

The little girl gazed at the calendar with wonder, her little fingers prying open the first two windows. Maggie saw a gold pear in one window and a little dog in another.

"It's Petit-four!" Mila said with wonder. She looked up at her mother and then Danielle. "How did the calendar know about Petit-Four? And that I like pears?"

Danielle beamed. "It is a very special calendar, *ma petite*," she said, kneeling down to kiss Mila's cheek. "I am glad you can see how special it is."

THE SECOND WEEK OF ADVENT

The next morning Maggie and Laurent were awakened by squeals of delight as Mila and Jemmy discovered their toy-stuffed sneakers.

Laurent groaned and pulled a pillow over his head.

"Those are the sounds of your precious children enjoying Christmas," Maggie said.

"Make them stop," he said in a voice muffled by the pillow.

Maggie kissed his neck and slipped out of bed. Laurent had not gotten to bed until well past three. The dinner had been a wonderful success but Laurent was incapable of leaving a dirty dish or wineglass sitting in the sink until the next morning. Maggie had long since come to terms with her own guilt at leaving him to it and going on to bed.

Pulling on a robe and jamming her feet into her slippers, she hurried out into the hall where Mila and Jemmy were seated beside a mountain of Christmas wrapping paper.

"*Maman!*" Mila squealed. "Pere Noël came last night!"

"I see he did," Maggie said. "Oh, my goodness. How well he knows you!"

Jemmy glanced up and narrowed his eyes at Maggie but then shrugged and went back to examining his toys.

That one is too smart, Maggie thought with a sigh. *He'll have Santa Claus figured out before he starts the first grade. Too bad. It's so nice to live in the fantasy for as long as you can.*

"Bring your toys," she said as she gathered up the wrapping paper and headed down the stairs. "Pere Noël's helper is still sleeping."

The children giggled at the thought of their large, six foot five papa as an elf and hurried down the stairs after their mother.

~

An hour later, the children fed and dressed, Maggie piled them into their Renault for a quick visit to the village. Maggie really only wanted to get the children out of the house for a little fresh air in order to give their father a moment to have his coffee in peace.

St-Buvard was small with only a very few shops in ancient buildings on its six-block main street. In the old days before children, Maggie would probably have met her best friend Grace on a morning like this to share a drink at Le Canard before walking the village's cobblestone streets.

But Grace was gone. In many ways long gone. Back in the States with her two daughters, she was attempting to put her life back together. Maggie only knew this because Laurent was still in touch with Grace's ex-husband Windsor. The few times Maggie had reached out to Grace had been met with silence.

Maggie shook off the memories and the ghosts—Madame Renoir's bakery, now a struggling bistro open only irregularly—and focused on the sound of her children's laughter. Jemmy was acting very much as if he'd drunk a case of Mountain Dew this morning. He knew what was coming in just two short weeks and could hardly contain himself.

Mila on the other hand, whether because it was just her nature or because she didn't yet understand what Christmas was about, was much more subdued. Maggie noticed the child still gripped the Advent calendar in her hand. Mila had pried open all the days up to and through the sixth which pleased Maggie because it meant she understood what the numbers were that Maggie had been teaching her.

There were very few people out this morning. The air was cold and raw although no snow had yet fallen. The proprietor of Le Canard, the main brasserie and pub in the village, was standing on his terrace and smoking. He nodded at Maggie as she and the children walked by.

At nine in the morning, it was still too early—even for Frenchmen—to be drinking *pastis*. Maggie had thought of stopping for coffee and hot chocolates for the children but had decided Jemmy wouldn't have the patience to sit still that long.

As they rounded the last corner before heading back to the car, Maggie spotted a figure bent over a trash receptacle. Instinctively, her hand shot out and grabbed Mila's hand.

"Jemmy," Maggie said tersely. "Turn around. Time to head back."

"Why? I thought we were going over the little footbridge on the other side? Please, Mama?" Without waiting for a reply, Jemmy quickened his steps toward the figure ahead.

"The footbridge! The footbridge!" Mila sang, jumping up and down.

Maggie kept a tight grip on the child and resigned herself to walking past the vagrant. Perhaps if they hurried...

"Mama, what is that man doing?" Mila asked loudly. The man lifted his head at the child's words and stared at Maggie. Jemmy hurried by him without even looking in his direction.

The man was elderly and unshaven. He was wearing the blue overalls known as *combinaison de travail* that had been ubiquitous in the rural parts of France decades ago. It was unusual to see anyone wearing them now. He also wore heavy work boots which looked old and worn.

His eyes held Maggie's.

In all her years of living as an expat in a small village, Maggie had long gotten used to the instant animosity that her alien status tended to trigger. It wasn't just the French, she reasoned. Most people in a small town were suspicious of strangers—or outsiders. But there was something different about the way this man was regarding her. It wasn't with the distrust or suspicion she normally expected.

It was with naked and abject sorrow.

His look seemed to wheedle its way into Maggie's bones like a cold draught.

"Mama, you're hurting my hand," Mila said and tugged away from Maggie's grip.

"Mila, no!" Maggie said as she watched in horror as Mila walked up to the old man.

"*Avez-vous faim, Monsieur?*" Mila asked in her high-pitched voice. "*Moi, je te donne une orange, oui?*" From her coat pocket, she pulled a small clementine she must have taken from the bowl in the kitchen at home and held it out to him.

Maggie sucked in a quick breath but was unable to do anything but stare.

The man closed his eyes and then bowed slowly. He held

out his hand, large and calloused, and Mila plopped the orange into it.

"*Merci, mon petit ange,*" he said in a low voice. *Thank you, my angel.*

"*Joyeux Noël, Monsieur,*" Mila said and then turned to catch up with Jemmy.

Maggie hurried toward the man, wondering if she should give him money and whether he would be offended?

As she walked by him, she smiled guiltily but gratefully too since the man had been kind to Mila. He nodded before disappearing into the dark alley behind him.

As Maggie walked behind her children, she considered whether she should scold Mila. After all, Mila had been taught never to approach strangers in any circumstances. On the other hand, Mila might well have believed the rule didn't apply because Maggie had been by her side.

"Mila?" Maggie called as they reached the wooden footbridge that spanned the tiny creek that marked the end of St-Buvard's borders. Mila had already run across the bridge and back again to wait for Maggie.

"*Oui, Maman?*"

"That was a nice thing to do back there with that man."

"Oh. You mean *Les Pauvres?*"

Maggie caught sight of Jemmy on the other side of the bridge clearly doing something muddy that would require Maggie to cover the seats of the car with newspaper before the child would be allowed in it.

"Why do you call him that?"

"Because that's his name, silly *Maman!*"

Maggie shook her head in befuddlement. "How in the world do you know his name?"

Mia held up the folded calendar that she still held in one hand. "Jemmy read it to me, that's how."

Maggie held her hand out for the calendar. Mila skipped the distance to her, unfolded the calendar and pried open the window over the day's date December 6.

There, behind the little opened window was an illustration of a beggar holding an orange. Underneath the picture were the words *Les Pauvres*.

THE THIRD WEEK OF ADVENT

That night Maggie slipped the calendar out of Mila's hands after the child had fallen asleep. There was no other way to interpret the illustration of the grizzled old beggar holding a bright orange than the way Mila had. The fact that neither Mila nor Jemmy knew that *Les Pauvres* was French for *the poor* was irrelevant. For whatever reason, Mila had felt prompted to bring the orange with her so that when she saw the homeless man, she had put two and two together. The child wasn't even amazed, Maggie thought.

It was as if life was all laid out in one perfectly logical and balanced storyline.

Maggie looked at the other windows of the calendar. None of them had been opened. Not only did that show amazing willpower on Mila's part but it meant that Maggie couldn't herself take a peek to see what else was coming.

"What is that you have, *chérie*?" Laurent said as he climbed into bed. "And can you turn out the light?"

It had been another busy day of cooking and preparing for the *réveillon* in two weeks' time for Laurent. Plus after last night's dinner party he'd definitely shown signs of a hangover for the first time since Maggie had known him.

We're getting older, she thought as she watched him settle into his side of the bed. This weekend would be another holiday party although it would feature less food and more wine—if that was even possible. Even so, because he was French there would always be food.

It was to be a major *degustation* for their wine label, *Domaine St-Buvard*. While most of the year's harvest had been destroyed, Laurent still needed to promote his label for next year and there was no better time to do that than at Christmas. Once more the house would have half the village milling about their living room. And because it was Christmastime, it would be all *the villagers'* friends and relatives too. Laurent's attitude was always *the more the merrier*.

"It's the Advent calendar that Danielle gave the kids," she said. "It's so weird, Laurent. There's a picture of a beggar under today's window in the calendar and today we met a beggar."

"It is a Christmas miracle," Laurent murmured. "The light, *chérie*?"

"In a moment." Maggie flipped back to look at the earlier little windows of the calendar. One revealed a bunch of grapes. One showed a cottage with smoke coming out of the chimney. The others seemed equally mundane.

She turned the calendar over and saw the other side where a feminine hand had scrawled *Noël 1950*.

Was this Madame Renoir's as a girl? Why had none of the little windows been opened? How had the calendar ended up in Jean-Luc's attic?

"Maggie..."

With a sigh, she dropped the calendar on her nightstand and leaned over to turn off the light.

She snuggled up against Laurent and he pulled her close and wrapped his arms around her. She listened to the sound of his heartbeat as she rested against his chest until his breathing evened and soft snores told her he was asleep.

On a night like this, she thought as she heard the wind rattle the shutters, with her whole family safe and snug inside, it was good to remember that there really was so very little to really worry about.

That week flew by in a rush of neighborhood visits—either people coming to Domaine St-Buvard or Maggie bundling up both children for trips to Aix where most of Jemmy's schoolmates lived. Next year she would need to decide whether Mila should start *l'école maternelle* or wait a year. She was certainly smart enough but while she wasn't shy, neither was she as social as Jemmy. Whereas Jemmy had been bursting at the suspenders to go to school and make friends, Mila was much more interested in solo play.

Maybe that's a reason right there to start her early at school? Maggie wondered as she drove back from Aix after a long day of two different Christmas parties and a birthday party. Both children were fast asleep in their car seats in the back. Maggie had insisted that Mila leave the Advent calendar in the car while they attended the parties. Glancing now in the rearview mirror, she could see that Mila held the calendar in her gloved hand as she slept.

In the days since meeting the beggar, the calendar pictures had produced nothing unusual. Laurent had gone into town looking for the beggar to offer him food, money and a ride to a shelter in Arles, but hadn't been able to find him. It had been odd to find a vagrant in St-Buvard. The village wasn't really on the way to any place and was so remote that if you didn't have a car, you'd never find it.

How did the old guy get there? Did he know someone in St-Buvard? Then why was he dumpster diving?

For the hundredth time, Maggie forced herself to put the man out of her mind. She had a million things to do to get ready for Christmas next week and for the back-to-back feasts she and Laurent would host for the *réveillon*. It surprised her how so much of her busyness had nothing to do with buying presents. With two small children, that job was easily and quickly done. Both kids were content—at least at this age—with relatively inexpensive trinkets. It was easy enough to fill the space under the Christmas tree with colorfully wrapped parcels and packages—most of which contained toys that would be broken or forgotten by New Year's Day.

The *degustation* last weekend had gone well—especially if you didn't count the two broken lamps and the chunk of ancient limestone taken out of their drive's entryway column by a couple of the villagers attempting to back out after three hours of nonstop wine sampling.

Maggie had found time to write her blog and get it off with all the felicitations of the season to her ten thousand subscribers—a number that never ceased to amaze her.

While she knew it was hopelessly old-fashioned, she'd even sent off a couple dozen Christmas cards—mostly to friends and family in the States. She'd included a chatty note to Grace but hadn't really expected a response and hadn't gotten one. Although even a printed "Best of the Season from Grace, Taylor and Zouzou" would have been better than nothing.

Mind you, Maggie thought. *It's early days. Something might still come.*

The St-Buvard Guild was having a small get-together tonight at Domaine St-Buvard. In Laurent's world, a "small get-together" still meant at least five courses. Maggie was sure she must have been mad to have volunteered to host it, but Danielle had encouraged her to do it.

She knew Laurent would charm the old ladies and all Maggie really would have to do was stay awake and smile in all the right spots and not say anything too overtly American. God forbid she would have to start the evening off apologizing for the new American president. And yet she feared that if she armed herself with a couple of cocktails beforehand—her usual method of international detente—she would fall asleep face down in the *ratatouille*.

As she pulled into the long driveway of Domaine St-Buvard, she noticed that the sun had dropped behind the large stone *mas*, bathing the side gardens in an alpenglow that made the vineyards look like they were on fire. These days she was usually so busy helping Laurent get dinner on the table and doing a million other things that she couldn't remember the last time she'd noticed that familiar sight.

She parked the car and the house front door flung open. Laurent must have been watching for her. As usual, her cellphone battery had died and she'd forgotten to take the car charger with her. If their roles had been reversed, she would have been seriously put out with Laurent but as he approached the car, little Petit-Four running at his heels, she could see his face was open and placid.

He went first to the back seat where he gently lifted Mila out without waking her and, with a quick smile to Maggie, he walked back into the house. Maggie tapped Jemmy's knee.

"Wake up, little man. We're home."

Jemmy yawned and blinked his eyes as he tried to wake up.

"Cartoons?"

Maggie laughed and they both got out of the car. "Why not? But keep the volume down. Your sister is sleeping."

When they got inside, Maggie saw that Laurent had put Mila on the sofa in the living room to finish her nap. However, she'd have to be woken, because the last thing anyone wanted was for Mila to sleep through dinner only to wake up at two in the morning starving and ready to start her day.

"She is already waking." Laurent assured Maggie as he took her coat and kissed her. "A good day?"

"An exhausting one," Maggie said. "Is it Easter yet?" She followed him into the kitchen, the sound of the laugh track for the cartoon show came to them from the living room. The kitchen clock already showed four o'clock. People would start to come at five. Maggie groaned.

"Go, *chérie*," Laurent said. "Take your bath. You have time even for a nap. Everything is in order."

"Are you sure?" Maggie asked, but she was already on her way toward the stairs. She could see the pots bubbling away on the stovetop and smell the aroma of garlic mingled with cinnamon and the evergreen of the Christmas fir in the dining room.

That night, Maggie was sure that Laurent had outdone himself. The *coquilles Saint-Jacques* were done in what the French call *entrée* sizes in small shells that Laurent served with a cold flinty Chablis. Most of the people in the guild were women and while Maggie better than most had reason to know how evil they could be, tonight—with Maggie's handsome *vigneron* husband waiting on them—they were positively simpering with pleasure.

Thankfully, Danielle was there to give moral support and while there were a few acidic comments about the new American president, Maggie was able to feign either deafness or a lack of understanding—even though it amazed her how after nine years the villagers could possibly believe she wasn't fluent in their language.

Laurent's amazing *blanquette de veau* helped too.

After a dessert of thick wedges from a massive Bûche de Noël that Laurent had bought at a patisserie in Aix, the ladies settled themselves in the living room with coffee and cognac. Maggie herself was awash with an intense feeling of contentment.

She knew it was totally the result of the wine and the cognac.

But still, it felt good.

That night, Maggie was so tired she thought she could fall into bed without washing a speck of makeup off or even taking off her earrings. She paused briefly in Jemmy's doorway to hear the child's breathing and then went to Mila's room.

She saw that Mila had fallen asleep with her little Lambie clutched in her arms and the calendar at the foot of her bed. It had been a few days since Maggie had checked the calendar. She picked it up and stepped into the light of the hallway.

She could hear Laurent washing up downstairs as she opened the little Advent calendar window for December 16. Underneath was a picture of a group of people holding hands across a dinner table. All of the people were different: brown, yellow, and white; some frowning, some smiling, some angry. Something stirred in Maggie as she stared at the picture and reflected on the unexpected camaraderie of the evening with the guild ladies who—regardless of how they often treated her—still considered her a part of their world. Maggie tried to tell herself that this was France and of course nearly every moment of significance could be illustrated as the coming together of friends and loved ones over a meal. It was in their culture, for heaven's sake.

But still, the other windows up to now had shown grapes or trees or old-fashioned shoes. And tonight—a picture that depicted a prickly group coming together to break bread and bond over the spirit of the season... Could this really be a coincidence?

THE FOURTH WEEK OF ADVENT

That final week before Christmas, Maggie was surprised that anyone in the country had an appetite left. She had feasted for so many days and nights that she was sure she was at least two pant sizes bigger than she'd been before Thanksgiving.

And they weren't done yet.

This week there were two more dinners—one tonight at Domaine St-Buvard and the other in two days at Jean-Luc and Danielle's farm. The dinners were part and parcel of the *réveillon*—the true feasting experience that was Christmas in France. Maggie had enjoyed the *réveillon* before, but never when it came in the final week of a marathon of gluttony. She was not entirely sure she would survive.

Laurent, of course, was totally in his element.

Because the *réveillon* was seven separate courses plus thirteen different desserts, he had been cooking for most of the days leading up to the dinner tonight at Domaine St-Buvard. After that, there would be two days grace—time to shop and cook and prepare in order to avoid showing up empty-handed at the second *réveillon* that would be at the Alexandre's.

Then, Maggie thought as she pulled on a pair of stretch pants that felt too snug, thankfully it would be Christmas Eve and the nonstop eating could finally end.

But after eight years of marriage to Laurent, she knew even thinking that was folly. There would, of course, be a massive Christmas Day lunch—for just the family and Jean-Luc and Danielle—and then New Year's Eve dinner and New Year's Day lunch.

After that, Maggie was determined she would subsist on lemon juice and fat-free yoghurt. But she knew she would have to smuggle the low-calorie yoghurt into the house. Laurent was categorically against anything he classified as "diet food."

As she glanced at herself in the full length mirror in the bedroom she grimaced and pulled on a heavy sweater that hung below her hips. Laurent would complain if only with a raised eyebrow, but—as Maggie had cause to know—his raised eyebrow could speak louder than another man's shouting.

She hurried downstairs to the accompaniment of the sound of cartoons in the living room. She poked her head in the room to see both children on the couch and their eyes glued to the antics on the television.

"Good morning, lovies," she said. Neither of them looked up. Mila sat transfixed, the calendar in one hand and her stuffed lamb in the other. Maggie sighed and turned toward the kitchen where the aroma of perked coffee warred with the strong smell of rosemary and garlic.

The *réveillon* was a big deal in France—or at least it used to be. And because it involved food, it was a big deal in Laurent's world too. The meal, whose name in French means *awakening*, was traditionally served by Catholic families either before or after Christmas Eve mass. These days it could take place at any time during the Christmas season and was really just an excuse to have a feast.

Maggie was reminded of her first Christmas in France when the village baker, Marie-Claire Renoir had created the traditional thirteen desserts for the *réveillon* when there was no-one in the village to buy them or care. Madame Renoir had been the first person to tell Maggie that the desserts had to do with the twelve apostles plus Jesus at the Last Supper. A wave of sadness swept into Maggie's thoughts as she remembered Madame Renoir.

But that's Christmas, isn't it? she thought. *It's not all shiny baubles and fruitcake. It's also memories of loved ones no longer with us and of childhood delights and expectations...long gone.*

She shook off her darkening mood and slipped onto the bar stool at the kitchen counter and reached for the mug of coffee Laurent had set in front of her. He turned to the stove and then pivoted to the counter where he was chopping shallots. For such a big man, he moved easily around his kitchen. Maggie was sure he could cook in this kitchen blind if he had to.

"Everything smells great already," she said.

"You will go into Aix today, yes? I have no time."

Maggie frowned. "Aix will be a zoo this close to Christmas."

Laurent turned and grinned at her. "This is not Wal-Mart. There will be no zoo. We French are moderate in our holiday observances."

"Sure, I see that. Although some would call it *non*observances. It's easy not to go crazy at the holidays if you don't believe."

"I do not know what that has to do with anything. You will go to Aix, yes?"

Maggie sighed. "Of course. What do you need?"

As Laurent outlined his list of *fromages* and pastries—a list Maggie knew for a fact would be written down and pressed into her hand before she left—she thought again of her parents and their plans for a beachy Christmas. She supposed it was the result of fifty years of holiday prepping —and expenses—that had them now thinking *what was it all for*? After all, her brother Ben could easily qualify as a veritable Scrooge for the holidays. No family of his own since the divorce and no religious affiliation to guilt him into pretending, he'd no doubt treat the whole month of December as if it were any other month.

A peal of laughter from the living room filtered into the kitchen.

Is it just because of the kids? Maggie wondered. *Is the only thing keeping all of us from just going to the beach on December 25 a bunch of little kids with wonder and innocence in their eyes? And once they're grown and gone so is the reason for the season?*

"*Chérie*," Laurent said, now standing in front of her, his hands on his hips and a dish towel thrown over one shoulder. "What is wrong?"

"Laurent, how did you celebrate Christmas before I came along? Before the kids?"

Laurent sighed and glanced at his watch.

"*Bien* sûr, *chérie*," he said, "I spent every Christmas waiting and praying for you to come along. If you leave now, you can go to the good *patisserie* on Cours Mirabeau."

If Aix-en-Provence Police Inspector Roger Bedard hadn't

spotted Maggie Dernier and her two children shopping in Aix this afternoon, he would never have thought to call Laurent to ask his favor. But he did see her.

He saw her looking more beautiful than she ever had before—which made him wonder briefly if she might not be pregnant again. She had a glow and a fullness about her that seemed to radiate down the street and illuminate all the lucky pedestrians and shoppers within her vicinity.

If the children hadn't been with her he would have approached her. They were friends after all. It was allowed. But greeting her with the children there to witness it would have taken so much more energy to pretend they were only friends—an exertion he chose not to make today.

No, he would call Dernier. Of course he would mention that he had seen Maggie in town—in Roger's experience it was always best not to lie if you didn't absolutely have to. And of course nobody had done anything wrong.

However, if thinking certain things was a crime, then naturally he was guilty.

Without doubt.

So he would call Dernier and wish him the joy of the season. It would be as simple as that. And while he knew Dernier owed him nothing, he also knew the man would attempt to make amends—even with no sin to be amended.

No sin except the fact that Roger loved Dernier's wife. Hopelessly, completely, uselessly.

Of course another Frenchman would completely understand that.

As he drove back to his office at the police station in Aix, he thought of his daughter Chloe and her tears to be allowed to go on a school trip to Morocco over Christmas.

What sort of school trip took children from their families over Christmas? he thought with frustration.

She was only ten and already she was trying to leave him.

Christmas Eve was in two days. An idea began to form in his head and Roger felt his pulse quicken. Tonight was not a major family event for anyone, he reasoned. Clearly Maggie was shopping for a feast of some kind. Probably the *réveillon*. It had not been since Roger was a child that he'd enjoyed a *réveillon*.

He changed his mind about calling Dernier to ask his favor.

Tonight he would go to Domaine-St-Buvard in person. He would bring Chloe so that they would be invited in.

And with Maggie there, surrounded by her children in her beautiful home, and Roger's own child by his side, well, Dernier would not dare to refuse him his request.

THE RÉVEILLON

That night of the Domaine St-Buvard *réveillon* was a dazzle of glittering lights and aromatic explosion to all the senses.

As Maggie stood in the kitchen taking from Laurent the serving dish of *sole meunière*—the fifth course in the menu—she tried to imagine how Mia and Jemmy were processing the event. She was proud that both children were behaving so well—especially since they were never allowed to stay up and join in with the adults for dinner. She was sure a few careful words from their papa was the reason. Laurent didn't spank the children—nor even raise his voice to them that Maggie had ever heard—but he had a manner that demanded obedience.

Tonight there was just the four of them and Jean-Luc and Danielle. There would easily be enough leftovers to stock the soup kitchen in Arles and Avignon. Maggie wasn't not quite sure where the extra food would go or why Laurent had cooked so much of it. As she turned to head back into the dining room, she heard the doorbell ring.

"Who in the world can that be?" she said, glancing at

Laurent. He was usually the reason for evening visitors, who were usually from his vineyard guild or contractors or other associates he never bothered to mention to Maggie.

Tonight he seemed as genuinely surprised as she was.

"Bring the fish in," he said, tossing down the dishtowel that had somehow found its way back to his shoulder. "I will see to the door."

Maggie came into the dining room where Jean-Luc was quizzing Jemmy on the names of the thirteen desserts. It was tradition that no child over five could have dessert until they had named them all correctly. Jemmy—always up for a challenge—had spent a good part of the week memorizing the desserts and was ready for his *Papere*.

"*Pompe à l'huile*," Jemmy said, pronouncing the words clearly in case Jean-Luc was hard of hearing but also showing off for Danielle and his little sister. "Plus two kinds of nougats."

"Ah," Jean-Luc said. "But do you know why there are two kinds?"

Jemmy frowned and glanced at his mother as if to ask if this was information he should have been given. Maggie smiled and spooned up the creamy sole onto his and Mila's plates and then handed the platter to Danielle. She could hear voices in the front hall.

"No," Jemmy said, narrowing his eyes at Jean-Luc. "Why are there two?"

"There are always the black and the white nougats," Jean-Luc said. "To represent good and evil."

Jemmy's face cleared. Maggie could already see him storing the information away for future use.

"*Bon*," Jean-Luc said. "What else?"

"Hazelnuts. Almonds. Raisins. Dry figs. Candied citron.

And…" Jemmy frowned as if in deep thought but before he could continue a group of people came to the dining room.

Maggie was surprised to see Laurent leading Roger Bedard and his daughter Chloe into the room along with a young couple. The couple looked frightened and their clothes appeared as though they had been worn for weeks. The woman wore a burqa. Her dark eyes darted fearfully around the room.

Maggie went to Roger and kissed him on both cheeks. She then turned to the couple.

"Good evening," she said. "Welcome. I hope you will stay for dinner? We have plenty."

The couple exchanged a look but said nothing.

Laurent was already bringing chairs in from the living room and parking them around the table. Jean-Luc shifted the dinner plates around to make room.

"I just told your husband," Roger said to Maggie, "I'm sorry to intrude."

"Not at all," Maggie said. "It's just family. No intrusion at all." She watched as Jean-Luc poured wine for the couple and handed a glass to Roger while Danielle went to the kitchen to get four more plates. She was already filling them as Laurent seated the couple.

"You've heard of the refugee camp near Aubagne?" Roger asked.

Maggie dropped her voice to a whisper. "The one that was dismantled? The one in the news? Are they from there?"

"They are. The area's done a fair job of re-housing a lot of the refugees but Hayyan and Rashaw here are a special case. And with Christmas coming, I would literally have to arrest them in order to give them shelter."

"A special case how?" *I swear if you tell me the woman's pregnant, I'm going out this minute to join a nunnery.*

"Hayyan has a criminal record. Nothing serious but enough to prevent immigration. He'll be shipped back to Syria as soon as we have the manpower.

"I'm sorry to hear that," Maggie said as she watched the young couple stare at the food on their plates.

"They need a place to stay," Roger said flatly. "Your husband…" He shrugged and didn't finish his sentence. Laurent joined them and motioned for Roger to take a seat.

He put a firm hand on Maggie's back and spoke in her ear. "I said they would stay with us as long as they need to. *Chérie*, did you put the bread in the oven?"

Maggie felt a strong rush of intense love for her husband —the man who did the right thing without a second thought—and she felt not for the first time the utter amazement that her life could have her joined with such a man. Her eyes moistened and as she and Laurent moved toward the kitchen to get the bread and slide a pan of stuffed mushrooms under the broiler, Maggie glanced at her children, now seated on either side of Roger's daughter.

Mila watched the young couple at the table with interest but with no obvious recognition of their significance. Maggie knew that was because the Advent calendar's picture of Mary and Joseph arriving at the inn wouldn't be revealed behind its little window for two more days.

CHRISTMAS DAY

It was the snow gently falling one hour after sun up on Christmas Day that made Maggie believe—truly believe—in miracles. When she was a child, there had been a few snowfalls in December in Atlanta but never on Christmas Day.

For Maggie, the squeals of her excited children as they raced to the living room rivaled the most beloved holiday carols for joy and delight. Laurent was already in the kitchen making coffee. Hayyan was with him. Not surprisingly, the man had taken to following Laurent around like a love-starved puppy. Equally not surprisingly, Laurent knew a little Arabic and the two men were actually able to communicate beyond pointing and nodding.

Separated from her husband, Rashaw seemed to overcome her initial timidity and became relaxed and friendly. Maggie was sure Rashaw was the stronger of the two. There was a lot of sadness in her eyes, no doubt because of everything she had seen and experienced. But she was young and life was long. So much goodness and joy could still be ahead for both her and Hayyan. Maggie prayed for that.

And of course in the few days that the couple had been with them, Rashaw had revealed that she was indeed expecting.

Not that Maggie was surprised. Not one bit.

"Mama! You got me the anti-gravity levitation kit!" Jemmy crowed. "M*oi, je l'adore!*"

Maggie smiled at him and watched as he and Mila foraged under the tree for more presents. Mila could recognize her own name when it was written on a tag. Her little Lambie tucked protectively under her arm, she carefully unwrapped her gifts as Jemmy ripped paper off willy-nilly.

"Oh, sorry, *Maman*," he said more than once when his unrestricted enthusiasm revealed a gift clearly meant for someone else.

"Please slow down, Jemmy," Maggie said. Laurent came into the room with a tray of steaming mugs. While Hayyan and Rashaw had very different cuisine preferences than the Derniers, one thing they all agreed on was coffee—and the stronger and hotter the better.

Laurent handed Maggie a mug and also her cellphone. "Your mother," he said before turning his attention to Jemmy and Mila.

"Merry Christmas, Mom," Maggie said into the phone. "What time is it there? Does Cabo have a different time zone than Atlanta? It must be three in the morning!"

"Well, darling, since we're in Arles, not Cabo, it doesn't matter what time it is there."

"You're in Arles?" Maggie's voice rose with excitement. "Are you serious? You're in France?"

"As long as Arles is still in France, then yes," her mother said and laughed. "Your father was able to rent the very last car in France before the whole country closed up last night. We told Laurent we'll be in St-Buvard in time for lunch."

After Maggie hung up she caught Laurent watching her and smiling.

"You didn't guilt them into this, did you?" she asked.

"I promise I had nothing to do with it."

Maggie believed him. Laurent would move earth and heaven for her and the children, that much she knew, but he would consider how and where his in-laws took their vacation to be none of his business.

"I can't believe it," Maggie said to herself.

"Your Mama?" Rashaw said to Maggie with a smile.

Maggie nodded. "Yes. I didn't think I would see them this year."

A sudden pounding on the front door startled them both but before Maggie could get to her feet, the door flew open and Jean-Luc strode through the stone foyer to the living room.

"*Joyeux Noël, mes petites!*" he said.

Mila squealed and ran to Jean-Luc, her eyes wide with wonder at the sight of the lamb cradled in his arms. Jean-Luc knelt and put the little thing on the carpet where it struggled to stand up. Mila instantly hugged the lamb and buried her face in its soft, thick fur.

Even Jemmy left his toys to run to the lamb. Petit-Four sniffed at the creature before trotting back to Maggie who stood with her mouth open in astonishment.

Jean-Luc shrugged off his coat. "I found it wandering in your back garden. Did you mean to leave it out?"

Laurent and Maggie looked at each other.

"Oh!" Jean-Luc said and handed Maggie a stack of envelopes. "You also forgot to pick up your mail." Maggie could see a thick envelope on the top of the stack.

She recognized Grace's handwriting.

"Mama! Papa!" Mila said still clutching the lamb. "It is

the last window in the calendar! It all came true! Lambie came to life just like the story said!"

You have got to be kidding me, Maggie thought as she put the stack of Christmas cards down, went over to her daughter and picked the calendar up from where Mila had left it on the carpet. Maggie opened the final window—December 25—and saw the illustration of a lamb in the manger with a halo of gold around its head.

She felt a warmth shoot up her hand from the calendar. It seemed to spread to her chest and infused her whole body with a glow as her very spirit began to rise. Her eyes misted as she thought of the young girl who had been given this calendar so many years ago. She thought of the snowy Christmas Eve when Marie-Claire Renoir had been only twelve—just before a sickening tragedy would change her life forever.

Thank you, Marie-Claire. Maggie thought, her eyes stinging with tears. She remembered Madame Renoir with her baker's hands covered with flour, her hair unsettled and wild around her head, and her eyes always searching for a different answer to her sad story.

But her innate kindness was always there—regardless of the horror and the madness. It was there when Madame Renoir gave Maggie Petit-Four as a puppy.

"Where is Danielle?" Maggie asked, turning to Jean-Luc and forcing the tears away.

"Oh, she's still in bed. I'll go back for her in a bit." Jean-Luc settled in a nearby chair with a mug of steaming coffee. "Laurent, what in the world made you think to give the children a live lamb for Christmas?"

Laurent shook his head as though he was still trying to process it all. "Monsieur Albert was to have delivered my order of lamb cutlets last night for our New Year's lunch," he said.

Monsieur Albert was Laurent's usual meat wholesaler.

"There was obviously a misunderstanding," Laurent said.

"That's putting it mildly," Maggie said as she sat down between Rashaw and her husband with the calendar still in her hand. "What are we going to do now?"

Laurent shrugged philosophically. "I suppose we will have roasted game hens instead."

Maggie wrapped her hands around her coffee mug and gazed out the French doors to the back garden as the snow drifted down outside. She thought of her parents just a few minutes down the road, of Grace finally reaching out to her, of Danielle and Jean-Luc—all beloved friends and family. She thought of the vineyard and how it gave Laurent joy and purpose, not to mention a livelihood. She thought of Rashaw and Hayyan so far from their own home—with no way back and an uncertain road ahead—and how grateful Maggie was that she could play a part in helping them. She thought of the richness of her life—the love, the comfort, the joy—all things she never dared to dream she might have some day.

Maggie looked down at Mila with her pudgy arms wrapped around the lamb and at Jemmy petting its curly head.

Thank you, Marie-Claire, for not opening the calendar when you got it. Thank you for hiding it and for somehow guiding it into Danielle's hands so that it might come to my family.

I pray you rest in peace, dear friend. I promise I will never forget you.

Then Maggie leaned back and let the joy of the moment

truly engulf her and all her loved ones on this snowy indescribably perfect Christmas Day in Provence.

Joyeux Noël!

HOLIDAY RECIPES FROM CHEF LAURENT

Here are the recipes for a few of Laurent and Maggie's favorite dishes around the holidays!

Coquilles Saint-Jacques
8 oz mushrooms, minced
6 TB unsalted butter
3 minced shallots
2 TB parlsey chopped
¾ cup dry vermouth
6 large sea scallops
2 dozen raw shrimp
1 egg
4 TB flour
½ cup heavy cream
2/3 grated Swiss cheese
Bread crumbs

Preheat oven at 350 degrees.
　　Boil scallops and shrimp in combination of vermouth and water. Remove shellfish, reserve broth. Sauté shallots

and mushrooms in butter. Make roue. (3 tablespoons butter, 4 tablespoons flour.) Cook roue until it's pale brown. Add shellfish broth and sherry.

Beat egg and cream in large bowl. Dibble hot sauce into it in a thin stream. When consistency is like a runny pudding, add scallops and shrimp and parsley. Pour into individual ramekins or one large baking dish. Top with grated Swiss cheese and sprinkle with buttered bread crumbs. Bake for 15 minutes or until top bubbles.

Aioli

2-3 peeled garlic cloves
1 egg yolk (room temperature)
2/3 cup (or more) premium olive oil

Pound garlic to a paste with a mortar and pestle (about five minutes.) Stir in egg yolk and begin to add the oil a little bit at a time. (You might want to switch to a food processor about now.) When the mixture begins to thicken, add salt and pepper.

If aïoli separates in the making, put it in a new, clean bowl. Clean the mortar and add a new egg yolk and begin again. Instead of pouring in oil, this time, add the existing (ruined) aïoli little by little until it reconstitutes.

Garlic Soup

While they might not do it any more, it used to be that French families began their meals with a hot cup of *Aigo-Boulido* (or, garlic soup).

Garlic cloves

Holiday Recipes from Chef Laurent

Olive oil
Bay leaf
Dried thyme
1 Egg
Toast
½ cup grated Parmesan cheese

Crush the garlic cloves in their skins and toss them into salted water with a glug of olive oil. Boil it all together for ten minutes and then add the herbs. Turn off the heat and cover for ten more minutes. Meanwhile, beat the egg into however many bowls you need for each person having soup and put a couple of pieces of really good bread down in the toaster or under the broiler.

Using a slotted spoon, remove and discard the garlic and herbs and pour the hot broth into each egg-bowl—beating each one as you do it. Tear off a solid piece of toasted bread (you can rub a piece of cut garlic on it if you like) and submerge in each bowl. Cover with the Parmesan.

Pot-au-Feu
1 pound beef tenderloin
6 cups chicken stock
2 carrots, sliced cross-wise
2 parsnips, likewise sliced cross-wise
1 leek, white part only, quartered
2 celery stalks, PEELED, and quartered
One fresh sprig each: thyme, rosemary, parsley

Brown the meat in a heavy pot over medium heat. Add all other ingredients and simmer for 30 minutes. Once the veggies are fork-tender, remove the meat to a cutting board using a slotted spoon. Arrange the veggies in four shallow soup bowls, ladle broth over them from the pot. Slice the meat and give each bowl two slices each.

Whip up mashed potatoes laced with horseradish and put a major dollop in the middle of each bowl.

Soupe de Poissons

2 lbs firm white fish (I use Tilapia but many recipes suggest bass or haddock or eel (?)
½-lb raw shrimp, boiled and shelled (save the water)
½-cup olive oil
1 tomato
Orange rind
1 onion, finely chopped
3 garlic cloves, crushed
White bread
Parsley, bay leaf, saffron, fennel
Parmesan cheese

Cut the fish into two-inch pieces. Put some heat under a big saucepan and add the oil, a few sprigs of the parsley, the chopped onion, 1 bay leaf, a pinch of saffron, the fennel, tomato, rind and the garlic. When it gets aromatic (sorry to be so nonspecific, but this is where your nose and your eyes work better than words—you're not cooking these items so much as you're marrying their flavors in preparation for the star of the show—the fish.)

Add the fish and cover with 1-1/2 quarts of the shrimp water. (If you don't have enough, top it off with regular spring water.) Salt and pepper it liberally and bring to a boil for 15-20 minutes. Turn off the heat and replace the wilted cooked parsley with another sprig of fresh parsley.

Ladle the soup into bowls.

Toast the bread and cut into squares or rounds. Put big healthy dollops of aioli on them and add them to the bowls so that they are bobbing on top. Grate fat curls of Parmesan cheese onto them.

Gourgères

These little jewels really are amazingly delicious and perfect for holiday entertaining. And, unlike many things French that are wonderful but take a bit of time to create, these can be happily stashed away in your freezer.

> 3 TB butter
> 1 cup all-purpose flour
> 4 eggs, chilled
> 1 cup Gruyère cheese, grated

Go ahead and preheat your oven to 400 degrees and line two baking sheets with parchment paper. Boil one cup of water with the butter and about 1 tsp of salt in a heavy but medium sized saucepan. Whisk with a wire whisk until the butter is melted and then add the flour—stirring rapidly with a wooden spoon—until the flour and the butter-water turn into a ball of dough that pulls away from the pot sides. Stir this ball around until it is no longer sticky—about 1-2 minutes. Take the pan off the heat and let the hot dough cool a few minutes.

Put the dough into your food mixer at this point so that you can add the eggs one at a time while the beaters are going. Also add the cheese and a few healthy grinds of pepper.

Use two spoons to drop the dough onto the baking sheets, about three inches apart. You might want to tamp down any "peaks" by wetting a finger and patting them gently.

Bake thirty minutes until golden brown but keep your eye on them. Be sure to turn the pan halfway through the baking time.

Transfer to racks to cool and serve them warm. If you're freezing them for use later, just drop them out—hard as fat marbles—onto another lined baking sheet and bring them back to life in a 350 degree oven for about 10 minutes.

***

Rouille

For those times when you need something hot and spicy you will need *rouille*.

6 cloves of garlic
2 egg yolks (room temp)
1 cup olive oil
¼-tsp saffron threads
Cayenne pepper

Peel and cut the garlic in half. Place in a mortar with a pinch of salt and start smashing. Once you've created a consistent paste, add an egg yolk and stir to blend. Repeat with the second yolk. Then—just like you do with mayonnaise or aïoli —start dropping the oil into the mortar drop by precious, gorgeous drop. Add the saffron and a pinch of cayenne.

Gradually whisk in the remaining oil in a slow stream until the sauce thickens to the consistency of pudding or mayonnaise. Taste and add cayenne as needed. Cover and pop in the fridge until you need it. And once you've made it, you'll be surprised how often you'll find yourself needing it!

Sole Meunière
¼ cup flour
4 sole fillets
4 TB butter
2 tsp lemon juice
1 tsp parsley, minced

Combine flour with salt, and pepper. Dredge each fish fillet in the flour mixture until well coated.

Melt 1 tablespoon butter in a large skillet over medium heat. Add the fish and brown 3 minutes each side.

Transfer to a platter and add remaining butter to pan and turn up the heat to medium-high.

When the butter starts to brown, add the lemon juice and parsley. Pour the butter over the fish and serve immediately.

Bon Appetit and *Joyeux Noël*!

A Provençal Christmas. A Maggie Newberry Short Story. Copright 2016 by Susan Kiernan-Lewis. All rights reserved.

A TURKEY AND SOME MISTLETOE

The village roads leading to Domaine St-Buvard gave no hint of the looming feast day. No twinkling fairy lights, no gaudy outlines of neon Christmas trees hanging from lamp posts—nothing to hint at the coming holiday.

And yet. There was a special undeniable feeling of Thanksgiving in the air for Maggie Newberry Dernier as she sat at the kitchen counter in her own French country kitchen in the *mas* she shared with her husband and two children on the outskirts of the French village of St-Buvard in Provence.

In fact, she was pretty sure that her own kitchen was undeniably the best thing about any holiday held at Domaine St-Buvard.

Especially since her husband Laurent was almost always in that kitchen.

Maggie leaned across the counter and watched him now as he stood in front of his pride and joy, the massive *La Cornue* stove that anchored the east corner of the small room. The scent of garlic, rosemary and sautéed shallots filled the air.

The kitchen counter around him was covered with bowls of sea scallops, Belgian endives, jumbo shrimp, garlic cloves and onions, fresh chives and a large block of butter—all ingredients for today's lunch and the beginnings of what would be their dinner.

It was the day before Thanksgiving with all the chaos and activity that that family holiday promised. But today that activity and expectation had been ratcheted up a notch.

Maybe two.

Today Maggie and Laurent were expecting overseas guests.

Just the thought of it made Maggie's stomach drop a little.

"Hey, just so you know," she said to Laurent, "*Gambas Flambées* with *pastis* is not traditional Thanksgiving fare."

Laurent glanced at his wife and gave a small smile. He was a man of few words at the best of times but when he was in his kitchen he was in a world that existed beyond words or idle conversation.

"Where are the kids?" she asked looking around as Laurent poured her another mug of coffee from the French press.

Their two children, Jemmy and Mila, ages ten and eight, even with dual citizenship, had never celebrated the traditional North American holiday anywhere but in France. There were times that Maggie, who was born and raised in Atlanta, Georgia, would have loved for her children to experience a traditional Thanksgiving in the country that invented it, but what with the grape harvest usually only just finishing up most years the timing had never worked out.

"They are collecting kindling," Laurent said. "When do you expect Grace and Danielle to arrive?"

Maggie's best friend Grace Van Sant ran a bed and breakfast owned by Laurent and situated on the other side of Laurent's vineyard. She lived there with her fourteen-year-old daughter Zouzou and their dear friend Danielle Alexandre who'd recently lost her husband.

"Grace said she'd try to get here early," Maggie said.

"So she will be late."

"I know! Right? Today of all days she needs to be here when she said she would."

Laurent raised an eyebrow at his wife. A handsome man and at six foot four unusually tall for a Frenchman, he was broad chested, taciturn and in Maggie's view, smoking hot.

"You have had too much coffee," he said.

"I never thought I'd hear a Frenchman say that," Maggie retorted. But she knew he was right. She was on her fourth cup and just the thought of who was about to walk through that front door was making agitated tremors shoot up both her arms.

"I honestly can't believe Windsor agreed to come," Maggie said. "What was he thinking?"

"He was probably thinking you invited him," Laurent said, turning back to his stove.

"I didn't mean for him to bring half of Atlanta!" Maggie said as she pushed her coffee mug away.

Windsor Van Sant—ex-husband of Grace—had responded with eagerness to Maggie's spontaneous and now fully regretted invitation to spend Thanksgiving in France at Maggie and Laurent's *mas* Domaine St-Buvard.

Unfortunately he'd also announced his intention to bring his new wife along with his daughter Taylor and her two-year old son.

"You should not have asked him if you didn't want him to come," Laurent said as he rinsed a colander of jumbo shrimp with their heads still on.

"How did I know he'd bring Taylor?"

Taylor Van Sant had been a problem since the day she'd entered the world. Feisty, truculent, very probably bipolar and with no evidence of affection or regard for any person in or out of the family, she'd recently topped her usual life's resumé of mayhem two years ago by getting pregnant from a one-night stand and then refusing to give the baby up for adoption—or agreeing to care for him herself.

With Grace living in France, Windsor and his new wife Susie had stepped in to raise the child.

"Remember the first time Taylor had Thanksgiving dinner with us?" Maggie asked.

Laurent turned and raised his eyebrow in disapproval,

"*Chérie*," he said. "As bad as Taylor was as a child, even you cannot lay murder at her feet."

A horn honked outside and Laurent turned to look out the kitchen window at the circular gravel driveway situated just outside.

"Please tell me that's Grace and Danielle," Maggie said.

"Looks like a rental car," Laurent said. "Ah yes. It is Windsor."

"Well, crap," Maggie said. "I'm going to kill Grace for being late."

"Meanwhile, *chérie*," Laurent said. "Let us go greet our guests."

THE WEATHER OUTSIDE IS FRIGHTFUL

I *officially hate Windsor's wife.*
Maggie sat across from Susie Van Sant with the coffee table between them in the salon at Domaine St-Buvard and smiled woodenly at her.

Susie Van Sant had probably been adorably chubby when she wasn't pregnant. But at six months, she was downright portly with a lumbering, swinging gait to go with it. She wore her dark hair cropped short which accented her double chin.

Not to mention the frown that went with it.

As soon as Windsor had hugged Laurent and Maggie and greeted Jemmy and Mila, he made the unnecessary announcement that Susie was pregnant.

And very pregnant. Maggie could not imagine how the woman had gotten onto a transatlantic flight at six months along.

As soon as Laurent had helped Windsor bring in all the luggage, Grace and Danielle pulled up behind Windsor's rental car. More hugs and kisses ensued until everyone was ensconced in the living room, a festive gin and tonic in one hand—lime soda for Susie—and the children back outside frolicking with Maggie and Laurent's large hunting dogs.

Laurent and Windsor had immediately gone to walk Laurent's vineyard—Laurent's favorite thing to do no matter the season. And Taylor had promptly retreated with her iPad and cell phone to her assigned guest bedroom upstairs.

Maggie hadn't seen Taylor in five years. Except for a few basics, the girl hadn't changed a bit.

Maggie decided that physically Taylor looked like she was trying out for the part of the girl with the dragon tattoo but that wasn't a surprise. Grace had brought back enough pictures of Taylor and the baby when she'd visited last summer so Maggie had known what to expect.

Taylor had always loved shocking people—and was usually only content if it was an unpleasant shock—so the fact that her head was shaved, her lips tattooed and pierced and her breasts nearly hanging out of what looked like a leather corset was to be expected.

Neither was it a surprise that Taylor paid absolutely no attention to her baby. Windsor and Susie alternated holding the boy until Grace showed up at which point they unceremoniously dumped him into her arms without bothering to hide their relief.

Clearly biracial, Zircon was bright-eyed and winsome. Maggie couldn't help feeling sorry for the little fellow—and not just for his terrible name. It was all well and good to be adopted by your biological family but if they were doing it largely for appearances sake, it was less than ideal.

And now that there was a "real" child on the way for Windsor and Susie, poor little Zircon didn't stand a chance.

Maggie hoped she was wrong.

"Maggie?"

Maggie turned to Grace who had just spoken to her.

"I'm sorry," Maggie said, blushing as if her uncharitable thoughts could be discerned by the expression on her face. "What?"

"Susie wants to know how much *Domaine St-Buvard* cost to renovate," Grace said sweetly.

In all the years that she'd known her, Maggie thought Grace Van Sant was still the most beautiful creature she had ever met. A clone of Grace Kelly but with her wit and charisma palpable from the moment she stepped into a room, Grace was a heavenly creature in every way. Maggie considered it extraordinary that Grace was still single since divorcing Windsor nearly five years ago.

"Sorry," Maggie said. "I have no idea. Laurent handles all that."

"Oh, that's right," Susie said, holding her hands primly in her lap. "Windsor told me you and Laurent have a traditional *French* marriage. I suppose that's from living over here so far from the States."

"What are you talking about?" Maggie asked.

"The *gougères* are superb, *chérie*," Danielle said as she handed the plate of cheese puffs to Maggie. "Have you had one?"

Knowing that Danielle was trying to forestall the line of questioning that Maggie now found herself determined to follow, Maggie took the plate and handed it to Grace.

"What do you mean *traditional*?" Maggie asked Susie.

"Just that you let your husband make all the important decisions," Susie said. "I suppose that might be a relief in some ways although I'm sure I could never do it myself."

"Laurent doesn't make all the decisions," Maggie said indignantly as a vein over her eye began to twitch. "And we don't have a traditional marriage. Why would Windsor say that?"

She glanced at Grace who was frowning and giving her best silent message of *will you chill out and stop rising to her bait?*

"Of course he's very forceful. Even I can see that," Susie said, picking nonexistent lint off her Betsy Johnson skirt. "And I suppose it's important to blend in and behave as the other French women do." She smiled condescendingly at Danielle.

Wow. It takes some skill to insult one woman and a whole country in one breath.

"I don't know what you're talking about," Maggie said hotly.

"Darling, you must take a turn with this precious cherub," Grace said suddenly plopping little Zircon on Maggie's lap. "What would the holidays be without babies?"

Zircon turned to grab Maggie's long hair and she came face to face with his serious little face. Instantly her heart began to melt. And when the baby grinned toothlessly at her, she let go of the rest of her irritation.

She turned to Susie and smiled.

"You must be so uncomfortable with all that extra weight, Susie. Can I get you another zero calorie soda?"

TINY TOTS WITH THEIR EYES ALL A-GLOW

Lunch was nothing less than an ordeal.

With Laurent in the kitchen surrounded by his "helpers" Mila, Jemmy and Zouzou, Maggie had been on the front line of attempting conversation with Susie and, worse, eventually Taylor herself when she finally deigned to come downstairs with a churlish announcement that she was ready to eat.

Lunch was a tense affair eaten in the dining room although Maggie had held out hope it might be warm enough to eat in the garden.

Traditional fare or not, the *gambas flambées* with *pastis* was a big hit. Even though Susie insisted that she didn't eat seafood, Maggie noted the woman enjoyed seconds and twice pushed the French fries bowl closer to her plate.

After lunch, Susie took a nap and Grace, still carrying Zircon around on her hip, attempted to reach out to Taylor. But Taylor retreated to her room for the rest of the day where she stayed until dinner.

Dinner—*Coquilles Saint-Jacques* because Laurent considered it a holiday dish and the children loved it—was much the same as lunch: delicious, deeply soul-satisfying and nearly unendurable.

Afterwards Susie, Maggie, Grace and Danielle all retired to the living room for an awkward hour of yet more stilted conversation until Grace and Danielle left early claiming a joint headache. Windsor was in the kitchen with Laurent and the children to help clean up, although how much cleaning Windsor was doing was hard to determine given the continuous laughter that could be heard from the living room.

Although Maggie had always been fond of Windsor, he had always struck her as a classic rich man. When she'd first met Grace and Windsor they'd just finished renovating a veritable castle on the other side of the village of St-Buvard. They'd spared no expense on the renovations or the furnishings and it had been photographed several times for various French and American home and garden magazines.

After the divorce it had taken a full three years to find a buyer for the property and even then Grace told Maggie that they'd had to sell for a fraction of what they'd put into it. Maggie had always wondered what the new buyers had done with the place—it had changed hands three more times since then. But Grace, who now lived just down the road from it in a humble stone cottage, said she didn't have the heart to look at it.

That night when she fell into bed, Maggie felt as if she'd run a marathon.

"Everything was delicious, Laurent," she said as she sat in bed in her Eileen West flannel nightgown and worked lavender salve into her elbows. "I can't believe we're already doing all this feasting and we're not even to Thanksgiving Day yet. At this rate I won't be able to fit into my aprons."

Laurent turned from where he sat on his side of the bed and gave her an askance look.

"Yeah, yeah," she said with a grin. "I know. I don't wear aprons. And speaking of which, what do you think of Susie?"

"Why do aprons make you think of Windsor's wife?"

"Because she thinks I'm a traditionally subservient wife who wears aprons and shines your shoes or something."

Laurent snorted.

"So, what do you think of her?"

He shrugged. "I think nothing of her."

"You don't have an opinion?"

"I haven't thought about it. I am understanding that you do have an opinion?"

"Laurent, she's awful! She's braggy and complaining and she hasn't looked at Zircon once since she got here."

"I do not know what that means," Laurent said. "The light, *chérie*?" He nodded at Maggie's bedside lamp.

"I hope she takes better care of him in Atlanta than she seems to here," Maggie said. "Grace carried him around all day today."

"Perhaps Grace is enjoying spending time with him since she usually does not see him. The light?"

Maggie snapped off the light and waited for her eyes to adjust as Laurent settled in the bed.

"Why did Taylor even come if she just wants to spend every minute in her room?" Maggie asked.

Laurent sighed.

"I mean, what's the point?"

"Go to sleep, *chérie*," Laurent said firmly, pulling her to him against his chest.

Maggie snuggled against him and felt some of the tension from the day begin to seep away.

But not all of it. Certainly not all of it.

HANG YOUR STOCKINGS AND SAY YOUR PRAYERS

Thanksgiving Day in Provence broke cold and clear. There was no snow yet but it wouldn't be far off if the sky could be believed. The cyprus trees that lined the drive to Domaine St-Buvard looked like spindly old men huddling in their overcoats to keep warm. And the branches of the oleander bushes in front of the kitchen window scratched the panes like they were trying to get inside where it was warm.

Danielle and Zouzou came over early but Grace had begged off with a continuing headache. She promised to be over before dinner.

Probably too much child care duty, Maggie thought. It's one thing to be a grandma for a day, quite another to be put on full-time baby duty.

By the time Maggie came downstairs, Laurent was busy frying pork sausage and flipping pancakes in the kitchen while Danielle, Windsor, Zouzou, Mila and Jemmy sat at the breakfast bar eating breakfast.

Two beautiful Calvados and *crème fraîche* apple tarts sat on the counter, evidence of Danielle's proficiency as a baker.

"Morning everyone," Maggie said, kissing Danielle. "Don't you know the first rule of preparing for Thanksgiving?"

"Is that the *starve yourself* rule?" Windsor said with baby Zircon on his lap, "so that you're good and hungry for the feast?" The baby was gnawing on a pancake without syrup.

"Exactly."

The pancakes did look amazing. Laurent handed her a mug of coffee with an expectant look.

"Yes, well, maybe just one pancake," Maggie said.

"They're the best Papa's ever made," Jemmy said.

Zouzou and Mila nodded enthusiastically. Maggie sat down at the counter next to Danielle who was just having coffee.

"So is Grace sick?" she asked Danielle.

"No, *chérie*. She just needed a little more rest."

Maggie glanced at Windsor who was busy chowing down on a stack of pancakes.

"Where's Susie this morning?" Maggie asked.

"Having a lie-in," Windsor said, turning to look at the baby. "Isn't she, Buddy? Mama's having a bit of a lie-in."

Maggie glanced at Laurent and raised her eyebrows.

Windsor refers to Susie as Mama to the baby?

A mildly scolding look from Laurent communicated the message as if he'd said it out loud: *It's none of our business. It's none of your business.*

After breakfast, Laurent stoked the fire in the living room and Windsor set up a portable playpen nearby into which he plopped Zircon.

Maggie noticed Zouzou was staying particularly close to Windsor which of course was perfectly natural. Since she lived in France, Zouzou rarely saw her father and she was still of an age to think her father was mildly wonderful.

Maggie hoped Windsor was keeping in touch with Zouzou throughout the year but then she heard Laurent's voice in her head: *mind your own business.*

Laurent invited Windsor to join him in the vineyard to collect more kindling and to see his new holdings. Since Danielle's husband had died the year before, Laurent had trebled the size of Domaine St-Buvard.

"Love to," Windsor said to Laurent as he watched Jemmy and Mila pull on their jackets to accompany them. "Hey, Zouzou, do me a favor, sweetheart?"

Zouzou turned to her father, a glowing smile on her face. Maggie thought this might be the first time Windsor had directly addressed his daughter since their initial greeting yesterday afternoon.

"Sure, Dad," Zouzou said eagerly. "What?"

"Can you mind the baby until your stepmom gets up? There's twenty bucks in it for you." Windsor tousled Zouzou's hair and turned to accompany Laurent and the other children outside.

Maggie wondered how old Windsor thought Zouzou was.

She was way past hair tousling.

Danielle and Maggie sat in the living room in front of the fire and Zouzou sat next to the playpen and watched her little nephew. Maggie couldn't read her expression but she didn't think it was particularly loving.

"This is the calm before the storm," Maggie told Danielle with a smile. "Once Laurent gets stuck into the full-on work of putting together the main feast of turkey, cranberries, and stuffing, I probably won't see him for the rest of the day."

"There is much to do on such a big day," Danielle said.

Maggie wondered what if anything she could say to

Zouzou to mitigate whatever it was the child seemed to be feeling. But after a few minutes, Zouzou put her headphones on and turned away from the baby who seemed content with playing with his stuffed toys in the playpen. Maggie could hear Zouzou's music but she checked herself from telling her to turn it down or she'd go deaf before she was twenty.

"Do you remember that first Thanksgiving?" she asked Danielle. "Here at Domaine St-Buvard?"

Danielle smoothed out the wrinkles of her crepe wool skirt.

"How would anyone ever forget? It was the day poor Monsieur MacKenzie died."

Maggie glanced at Zouzou to see if she'd heard but she didn't detect any reaction.

"Yeah, in our basement." Maggie shivered involuntarily at the memory.

"It was a terrible day," Danielle said.

"It truly was. My parents were here that day. And my niece, Nicole. Grace and Windsor were still married. And little Taylor. Do you remember Taylor as a small child?"

"She was hard to miss."

"Yeah, she was a pain even then. Grace once told me that she thought twice about having more kids after they had Taylor."

"She should not have shared that with you."

"Probably not."

They were silent for a moment listening to the fire crackle in the hearth. Maggie knew Danielle had a special affinity with Zouzou. All the kids considered *Mamère* their beloved grandmother. But Danielle was closest with Zouzou, who was often in the kitchen with Danielle baking and creating recipes. For Danielle, Zouzou was the child she'd never had. Just the thought that Grace might have decided not to have her must be harrowing to Danielle, Maggie thought.

"Unfortunately from what I can see," Maggie said, "Taylor hasn't changed."

"One thing I have learned in my sixty-eight years," Danielle said, "is that your best chance to be happy lies in letting go of what you think you know about the past."

"You mean like not judging Taylor based on who she was as a kid?"

Danielle looked over at Maggie and seemed to come out of her reverie. She smiled.

"*Exactment, chérie.* It is not wise to make judgments today based on how things used to be."

A few minutes later, Zircon had fallen asleep and Maggie could see through the French doors that the outdoor group was heading back to the house with arms full of kindling and firewood. She glanced at her watch. They'd been gone for nearly forty minutes and Susie still wasn't up.

Not that Maggie was eager to see the woman. In just a single day she'd already fallen into the habit of acting like Maggie was her servant and that the Domaine St-Buvard kitchen was a full-service French restaurant where no money changed hands.

"Oh, *chérie*," Danielle said. "Did you finish that book I loaned you last month? Madame Dulcie in the village wants to borrow it."

"Oh, yes, I did," Maggie said as she stood up. "It was great. I loved all the references to World War II and this area. Madame Dulcie lived it so she'll really appreciate it. It's just upstairs in my bedroom. Let me get it now so I don't forget."

Maggie hurried up the stairs to the floor the bedrooms were on just as the garden French doors opened and Laurent and Windsor and the children filled the annex next to the dining room.

When Maggie reached the top of the stairs she paused for a moment and heard Zouzou talking excitedly to her father. Maggie hoped that Windsor intended to give the girl some special time during his visit.

She walked down the hall toward the bedroom she shared with Laurent and as she passed Taylor's door she slowed and then stopped.

Inside she could hear music and then Taylor talking. Assuming she must be on the phone, Maggie listened in spite of herself. Taylor's voice was sarcastic and contemptuous.

"...*I wouldn't have even come if my dad hadn't promised me a thousand bucks to do it. No, seriously. It sucks so bad here."*

Shaken, Maggie stepped back from the door and continued toward her room.

Why would Windsor pay Taylor a thousand dollars to come? It might make sense if Taylor was taking care of her own child but she had totally ignored Zircon since arriving.

As Maggie came to her own bedroom door and reached for the door handle, she realized the door was ajar. She was sure she'd closed it before coming down to breakfast. Stepping into the room, she immediately noticed the glittering of gold on the floor in the patch of sunlight coming through the floor to ceiling window.

She bent down and found one of the emerald and diamond earrings that Laurent had given her for their last wedding anniversary. For a moment she touched her ear thinking it must have fallen out, but she was wearing her pearl studs this morning.

She then noticed her closet door was also open.

With a roiling stomach and a slight tremble of chills up her arms, she opened the closet door and saw her jewelry box on its side with its lid open and earrings, gold chains and bracelets falling over the rim and onto the floor.

Someone had been in her jewelry box.

THE FIRE IS SLOWLY DYING

Her gold bracelet was gone. With mounting panic and shock, Maggie carefully went through her jewelry box, sorting out the earrings and bracelets, picking up the ones that the thief had carelessly spilled out onto the carpeted floor. The only thing missing was a twenty-four caret gold Bismark bracelet.

It had belonged to Maggie's grandmother who'd given it to Maggie's mother who had handed it down to Maggie last Christmas.

Maggie staggered to the bed and sat down with legs that would no longer hold her.

Someone came into my room and stole the bracelet.

Her mind was whirling with how this could have happened, *when* it could have happened and more importantly *who could have done it.*

It has to be Taylor. She's right across the hall. She's motivated by money or she wouldn't even be on this trip.

And while Maggie had not heard of any reports of Taylor stealing before—in fact now that she thought of it

Grace had been remarkably close-mouthed about Taylor recently—the girl had done just about everything else and it wouldn't be a very big step to larceny.

But why?

Surely she's not so stupid not to know I'd find out?

Feverishly Maggie's mind worked on deciphering the mechanics of how she could confront Taylor.

Should I search her room first?

And then she thought of her house full of guests and the blowback from her accusing Taylor of stealing the bracelet.

Should I go to Windsor? Grace?

She ran a hand through her hair and stared at her closet door, so transfixed on what she should—or shouldn't do—that when Laurent came into the room and spoke her name she jumped.

"Oh!" she said, a hand flying to her chest. "You startled me."

Laurent frowned and looked around the room.

"You have guests downstairs," he said. "Danielle said you came up to—"

"Yes, yes," Maggie said, going to the bookcase and snatching up the book. "I'm just coming down now."

"You are all right, *chérie*?" Laurent asked.

"Yes, of course," Maggie said. "I'm fine." She gave him a quick kiss on her way out and hurried down the stairs wondering why her first instinct was not to tell him of the theft.

What could she possibly say that wouldn't ruin his Thanksgiving?

Oh by the way, I think Taylor came into our bedroom this morning and rifled through my jewelry box. Pass the gravy please.

No, she needed time to think about the situation and

think carefully about what she should do about it. She knew she had a tendency to react too quickly.

With a house full of friends and family and emotions already on high alert, now was not the time to jump to conclusions.

Except, who could it possibly be besides Taylor?

LET NOTHING YOU DISMAY

Thanksgiving dinner minus six hours and counting.
While pancakes may have been encouraged at breakfast, even Laurent knew to hold back until the actual feast hour approached and he closed the kitchen to anyone not peeling potatoes or washing pots.

Grace came over just before eleven and looked washed out and wan but of course still beautiful. Maggie hadn't noticed any interactions between Grace and Windsor yesterday. Theirs had been an acrimonious divorce with copious threats and insults flying back and forth—compounded by a couple of unfortunately romantic liaisons on Grace's part that had sufficiently blotted her copybook as far as winning any mother of the year awards.

Maggie knew Grace was still deeply ashamed of her behavior and had worked steadily the last two years to repair her relationship with both her daughters. Zouzou was fine now but Taylor had rebuffed every overture to reconnect from Grace.

Maggie led Grace into the living room where Danielle and Susie were watching the baby in his playpen.

"Can I help?" Grace asked throwing a longing look toward the kitchen where everyone could hear Windsor's booming laugh.

"Too many cooks," Maggie said. "Laurent's orders."

"I can't imagine Windsor is actually helping," Grace said as she sat down. "Except maybe by providing the entertainment."

"You don't know him as well as you think you do," Susie said tartly, eyeing Grace with a jaundiced eye as she languidly rubbed circles on her protruding belly.

"And thank God for that," Grace replied sweetly.

"The fragrance of the turkey is divine," Danielle said, clearly attempting to interrupt whatever was brewing between Grace and Susie. "*Le dinde* is not a common dish in France."

"I'm pretty sure Laurent had to order it a month ago," Maggie said, glancing at the stairs and wondering for the hundredth time if Taylor ever intended to come down. Maggie had made up her mind that she would confront the girl. She just wasn't sure of when.

"Personally I do not care for turkey," Susie sniffed. "Windsor always has them prepare a ham for me."

Who's them? Maggie couldn't help but wonder. *Do they have servants? A cook?*

"Laurent makes a sort of lamb meatloaf thing too," Maggie said.

"I detest lamb," Susie said.

Of course you do.

"Well, there's always bread and butter," Grace said cheerfully. "And nobody does it better than France." She turned to Maggie. "I hear Zouzou in the kitchen. Where's Taylor?"

"She has a headache," Susie said, surprising Maggie. She hadn't heard that Taylor had a headache. It occurred to her that Susie just made that up because she needed Grace to know that *she* was more in tune with her daughter than Grace was.

When will this day be over?

An hour later and Jemmy and Mila let the dogs out and joined them in the garden for a romp in the vineyards. Grace wandered into the kitchen to see if she could help and Maggie bundled up Zircon to join Mila and Jemmy outside. Danielle offered to come too. Susie waved away any and all invitations to budge from where she sat in front of the fire place.

Maggie and Danielle walked into the garden. It was cold and the leaves were wet from the rain they'd had the day before. Maggie was glad the dogs and children were getting a chance to run outside.

While there would be no marathon football on the TV to collapse in front of, she knew the rest of the day would still be spent largely indoors in front of the TV. They should all get a little fresh air while they could.

"Do you think I should put the baby down?" Maggie asked. "I'm sure he could use the exercise but I don't know how steady on his feet he is."

"I'm sure the fresh air is enough," Danielle said, tweaking Zircon's fat little cheek.

"We've had a theft," Maggie blurted out.

Danielle frowned. "Where? The village?"

"No. Here. Someone broke into my room and stole a gold bracelet."

Danielle sucked in a gasp. "Oh, *chérie! Non!* What has Laurent done about it?'

"I didn't tell him yet."

Danielle frowned. "Why not?"

"Think about it, Danielle. It's obviously Taylor. Who else could it be?"

"*Chérie*, that is dangerous thinking. Are you sure you didn't lose it yourself?"

"My jewelry box was on its side with half its contents on the floor."

Maggie was about to call the children back—they were running far ahead and she no longer see them. She heard the dogs barking in the distance over the next rise.

"Don't say anything to Grace," Danielle said.

"I won't. She has enough guilt without knowing Taylor robbed me too."

"Try not to jump to conclusions."

"How can I not?" Maggie said in exasperation. "Name me one other person it could be."

Danielle shook her head and shivered in her great coat. "I do not know. But I know you have the power to destroy this day for all of us if you are not careful."

"Me? Isn't the person about to destroy this day the one who stole the bracelet?"

"No, *chérie*. Most definitely not. And I think you know that."

O'ER THE FIELDS WE GO

Once back in the house, Maggie helped Grace settle Zircon down for his nap upstairs in Susie and Windsor's room while Laurent directed the children to set the table. He'd had Jemmy cut pine boughs yesterday morning. Zouzou and Mila fitted them now around each of the fat candles set in a row down the middle of the white linen tablecloth.

Maggie knew Danielle was right. If she said nothing everything would go on smoothly and everyone would have a pleasant Thanksgiving.

Or as pleasant as possible given the fact that Susie and Taylor are both here.

But as soon as Maggie even hinted to Taylor that she knew what she'd done, there was going to be an altercation and it was going to be big enough to blow the whole day out of the water.

Not unlike the Thanksgiving thirteen years ago, Maggie thought—the day Connor MacKenzie ended up strangled and stuffed in a wine cask in the basement of Domaine St-Buvard.

"Are you all right, darling?" Grace asked as they tiptoed back down the stairs.

"Fine. Somebody just walked on my grave is all."

"Oh, darling. You and your quaint Southern sayings. You should write a book."

"Have you had a chance to talk to Taylor yet?"

"Oh, several," Grace said airily. "Unfortunately *she* hasn't had an opening in her busy schedule. I'm sure I'll connect with her before she leaves."

Grace didn't at all sound sure. She sounded resigned.

"What about Windsor?" Maggie asked. "Have you talked to him?"

Grace frowned, one hand on the banister poised to make her descent.

"Why would I? We've agreed on child support. There's nothing more to say."

Except Maggie knew that half the reason Grace had wanted Windsor to come for Thanksgiving was that she was hoping they could get back on track—at least to the point where they could have a civil discussion. After all, they still shared two children together.

When they reached the bottom of the stairs, Laurent was waiting for them.

"Do you need me?" Maggie asked, astounded that that might be the case.

"Not for the dinner, *non*," Laurent said as he slipped an arm around her waist and pulled her close. He kissed her ear. "But for other things, *bien sûr*." Then he released her and turned to Grace "A word?"

Grace and Laurent grabbed coats off the peg in the foyer and stepped out the front door. Maggie knew there was a plumbing issue at one of the cottages at Grace's *gîte* that Laurent wanted to have his man look at.

"She's just getting more and more brazen, isn't she?" Susie said as she waddled over to where Maggie was still standing at the foot of the stairs.

"What are you talking about?"

Maggie felt a pinch of anger but she knew that's what Susie was striving for and she fought not to let it develop. The fact that Grace and Laurent had stepped outside was less a need for privacy and more because Laurent was likely ready for a cigarette.

"Oh, come on. It's happening right under your nose," Susie sneered. "Your best friend and your husband?"

"You're demented."

As soon as she said it Maggie knew she shouldn't have. Not because it wasn't nice but because it made Susie think she'd hit a nerve.

Susie smiled and rubbed her stomach faster and faster like she was trying to conjure up a genie.

"That woman has absolutely no loyalty," Susie said. "Not to you, not to her husband."

"You mean *Windsor*? He's not her husband any more. You of all people should know that. Oh, gosh! You're not saying that Windsor is stepping out on you?"

Susie flushed angrily. "Don't be ridiculous. That's not what I'm saying at all."

"Because I'm sure he's probably over Grace by now. Well, *maybe*. I mean she *is* gorgeous. Who could be married to her and ever really get over her? Know what I mean?"

"My husband...Windsor wouldn't...he couldn't..."

"Hello, girls," Windsor said jovially as he stepped out of the kitchen rubbing his hands together. "Almost ready for some turkey and gravy?"

"You know I hate turkey!" Susie shrieked at him with

eyes protruding and her chin held high before stomping off to the dining room.

Windsor watched her go, his mouth open in dumbfounded shock.

"What'd I say?" he said, blinking rapidly.

The moment Windsor turned to hurry after his wife, Maggie heard the footsteps on the stairs behind her. She turned to see Taylor coming down the stairs, an insolent scowl on her face. She didn't even glance at Maggie but looked toward the kitchen.

"I'm hungry," she said. "Where's lunch?"

You mean Thanksgiving dinner? Maggie wanted to say.

"Almost ready, I think," Maggie said instead. "Did you sleep well last night, Taylor?"

"What?" Taylor said, her face screwed up at having to converse with Maggie. "Where's Susie?"

"She and your father are in the dining room," Maggie said as the front door opened and Grace and Laurent came inside. A blast of cold air came with them.

"It's freezing out there!" Grace said and then spotted Taylor. "Oh, hi, Taylor. You're up."

"Why does everyone act like it's such a big deal that I'm up?" Taylor said grumpily, turning to walk into the dining room. Grace hurried after her.

"You need me for anything?" she asked Laurent.

"We'll sit down in thirty minutes," he said, then patted her shoulder before retreating back into the kitchen.

Maggie turned and ran up the steps, her heart pounding in her throat. From the minute she saw Taylor on the stairs she knew that this was the moment she'd been waiting for.

A confrontation with the girl could only end it acrimonious denials and recriminations and would get her nowhere.

But evidence was undeniable. Evidence was what Maggie needed before she confronted Taylor.

The door to Taylor's bedroom was open a crack and Maggie quickly pushed it all the way open. She scanned the room. They had moved Mila into Jemmy's room so Taylor could have the room all to herself.

Mila's room was the smallest bedroom in the house but it was cozy and had been decorated to look like a princess's boudoir. Mila's twin bed had a canopy of eyelet and flounce and was covered with stuffed animals and frilly pillows. A painted white armoire served as her closet and a toy box against the wall held her dolls, puzzles, books and little boxes of costume jewelry.

But now Taylor's clothes were draped over the bookcases and the headboard, her dirty clothes were on the floor where she'd stepped out of them and there were dirty dishes to show she'd obviously raided the refrigerator last night and brought her food upstairs.

Good thing she didn't take anything that Laurent had plans for, Maggie thought, *or we'd have our second Thanksgiving Day murder in this house.*

Maggie paused to try to hear if she could sense anyone coming upstairs over her pounding heart. All she heard was the hum of people talking on the floor beneath her. She went to Taylor's suitcase. She'd already decided that if anyone came in she'd just say she was looking for something that belonged to Mila.

On the other hand she knew it might be a little tricky getting anyone to believe that when she had her hands plunged deep into Taylor's suitcase.

She worked quickly. She checked the side gussets of the

suitcase and ran her hands along the shoe pockets. She checked under the bed and even under Taylor's pillow but there was no bracelet.

Suddenly she thought of Taylor's backpack. She spotted it nearly crammed underneath the bed. She picked it up and pulled out a laptop. Earphones fell to the floor. She hurriedly jammed her hands into the deepest recesses of the bag, her fingers feeling desperately for the feel of the heavy gold bracelet.

She pulled out pens, a SIM card, a USB key and a pack of American cigarettes with matches jammed into the cellophane sheath.

But no bracelet.

"What the hell are you doing in my room?"

BABY, IT'S COLD OUTSIDE

Maggie turned to see Taylor standing in the doorway with a look of outrage on her face.

"What are you doing?" Taylor said loudly, stomping into the room and snatching her book bag out of Maggie's hands. "Are you looking for drugs? Because I don't have any."

I never even thought of drugs.

"I'm looking for a seven-inch twenty-four caret gold bracelet," Maggie said, watching Taylor closely. She knew most thieves wouldn't be able to help glancing at wherever they'd hidden the stolen object.

Taylor glared at Maggie, her face reddening.

"And you thought I took it?"

Maggie was horrified to look over Taylor's shoulder and see that both Windsor and Susie had appeared in the hallway.

"What's going on?" Windsor said with an unsure smile.

"Your *friend* here is accusing your daughter of theft!" Susie said shrilly but with what Maggie could have sworn was a twisted smile of triumph on her face.

"Surely, not," Windsor said but his eyes were on Maggie and he didn't look at all sure.

"All I know," Maggie said, feeling her own confidence erode in the face of three people standing their ground against her, "is that someone knocked over my jewelry box and took a gold bracelet."

Oh, God, I did look everywhere, didn't I? Under the bed? In among my shoes? Could this all be a mistake? But then who knocked the jewelry case over?

"That's it!" Susie said smugly. "Windsor, pack our bags. We're leaving."

"You can't be serious," Windsor said helplessly looking from Susie to Maggie.

"What's going on?" Grace said, appearing in the hallway.

"Your *friend* here just accused Taylor of stealing her jewelry," Susie said sharply, wheeling on Grace.

Down the hall Maggie could hear Zircon awake and begin to cry.

"Well, did you?" Grace said turning to Taylor.

"Why does that not surprise me?" Taylor screamed at her.

"Lower your voice!" Windsor bellowed. "You'll wake the baby!"

The baby began to scream in earnest now and Maggie knew exactly how he felt.

"How can we possibly stay here?" Susie said. "Taylor said it would be like this but I just couldn't imagine it was going to be this terrible."

"Taylor said that?" Grace looked at Windsor. "Helping our daughter hate her own mother, Windsor?"

"I never said anything to her!" Windsor said angrily.

Maggie saw Jemmy, Mila and Zouzou appear from

behind Grace. *Where was Laurent if his sous-chefs were allowed to be AWOL?*

"You guys go on downstairs," Maggie said to them. "The adults are sorting something out."

"We're sorting out hypocrisy and discrimination," Susie said waspishly.

"Don't tell them that," Grace said to her. "They're used to *believing* adults. We haven't gotten around yet to telling them that some adults are total idiots."

"How dare you!?" Susie roared, her face mottled unattractively and her fists clenched at her side.

"Darling, calm down," Windsor said. "I'm sure this all just a misunderstanding."

"Maggie was going through my things," Taylor said, "because she was so sure I'd stolen her stupid bracelet. This is worse than *Orange is the New Black*."

"Look, I'm sorry," Maggie said, her cheeks burning. "I mean, of course if you are innocent I am beyond mortified that I—"

"*If I am innocent?*" Taylor said. "What's it going to take to prove it to you? Somebody else confessing?"

"Or perhaps finding it in *your* room," Susie said to Maggie. "Shall we all go into your room, Maggie, and help you find it?"

There was literally nothing Maggie wanted to do less.

Unless it was to then have Susie or Taylor find the bracelet in her bedroom.

She wouldn't put it past Taylor not to have it stuck up her sleeve.

Laurent suddenly appeared behind Grace, a look of questioning on his face but his eyes were on Maggie in an unmistakable *what have you done?* look.

Grace turned to get Zircon who had either calmed himself down or succeeded in screaming himself breathless.

"Well," Maggie said brightly, pushing out of Taylor's bedroom and smiling bravely at Laurent as she squeezed past him in the hall. "I'll just bet it's time to sit down to Thanksgiving dinner," she said hurrying down the hall.

JACK FROST NIPPING AT YOUR NOSE

Taylor and Susie sat next to each other and across from Danielle and Grace who sat with Zircon in his high chair between them. Maggie didn't have the heart to even glance at Danielle because she was pretty sure she'd see the disappointment in Danielle's face that Maggie hadn't taken her advice.

Susie snapped out her napkin and spread it ostentatiously over her baby-mound, her eyes narrowing at Grace as if *she* and not Maggie were the cause of the present brouhaha. Maggie sat at one end of the table with the children scattered between her and Laurent who stood at the other end with his back to the kitchen. The roast turkey glistened on a platter before him.

Laurent was one more person—beside Danielle, Taylor and Susie—who Maggie wasn't totally comfortable looking in the eye at the moment.

Could I have been wrong?

"And furthermore," Susie said abruptly, "Taylor couldn't have stolen your bracelet because she was with me the whole time."

"Susie," Windsor said, shaking his head.

"Someone stole your bracelet?" Jemmy asked, his eyes wide and looking immediately at Taylor.

"Why are you looking at me, you little punk?" Taylor snarled at Jemmy.

"Taylor," Laurent said.

All imaginable threats and foreboding lived in that one word, especially the way Laurent said it. And Taylor knew it. She'd crossed swords with Laurent before. Once when she was younger. And stupider.

Now she looked at him, her face ablaze with emotion.

"I didn't steal the stupid bracelet. But nobody ever believes me."

"Maybe there's a reason for that," Zouzou muttered into her chest.

"Look," Maggie said, holding up her hands to get everyone's attention. "This is my fault and I am so sorry for it. Taylor, I'm sorry. I should never have gone into your room. I apologize."

Taylor shrugged and looked down at her plate.

"I know how this is," Susie said imperiously. "It's because Taylor used to be a handful so you and Grace can't get over that she's changed. That Windsor and I have been such a positive influence on her. We did what Grace couldn't do."

Maggie's face reddened and she chanced a glance at Laurent who very imperceptibly shook his head.

"Is that why Taylor was only arrested for possession instead of dealing this year?" Grace said. "Your positive influence?"

"Grace!" Windsor said. "I told you to keep that to yourself!"

"I did, Windsor. I kept it even from my best friend. Maggie had no idea that Taylor did eighteen months for possession. She had no idea that Taylor was arrested for stealing a car *twice* last summer and that she's currently out on bail for..." Grace hesitated and glanced at Zouzou. "Close your ears, Zouzou. You too, Jemmy and Mila."

All three children slowly put their hands over their ears.

Grace lowered her voice. "For prostitution," she hissed. "Maybe that's why Maggie still invited her for Thanksgiving anyway because she *didn't* know the truth. How I wish now I'd told her. Don't you dare apologize, Maggie. There's no doubt in my mind that Taylor stole the bracelet."

"Are you finished, you dragon?" Taylor yelled.

"Leave the table," Laurent said. The vibrations of those three words were felt in every person seated. Taylor stood up, her chair knocking back onto the stone pavers of the dining room.

"With pleasure!" she said.

"If she's not welcome at this table, then neither am I!" Susie said, tossing down her napkin and then struggling to get out of the chair. Windsor stood to help her out and she slapped his hands away.

Once standing, Susie turned on Grace.

"There's no doubt in my mind that you are the reason for all of Taylor's problems," she said.

Maggie knew there was nothing Susie could have said that would hit home more precisely—or painfully—than this. Grace already blamed herself for Taylor.

"Windsor has given everything he has to that child," Susie said, her face flushed dark red. "He's focused all his money and attention on her. But soon there will be a second child and he needs to refocus his attention on this one."

"There already is a second child," Grace said coldly.

"What?" Susie looked confused and placed her hands on her belly.

"I said Windsor already has a second child."

Susie screwed up her face. "What are you talking about?"

But by then Zouzou had burst into tears and fled the table.

Grace got up to go after her and Windsor turned to help Susie up the stairs.

Jemmy looked up at Maggie.

"Gosh Mom I thought we were supposed to treat our guests like company not accuse them of stealing."

Thirty minutes later everyone had reassembled at the table minus Taylor and Susie. The Thanksgiving prayer was said, sounding much too ironic for Maggie's comfort, the turkey was carved and the dressing and all the trimmings passed around.

A pall hung over the table in spite of Zircon's adorable and distracting antics.

Once when Maggie slipped into the kitchen to get more gravy, she felt Laurent behind her.

"I am eager to hear the whole story when I get you alone later, *chérie*," he said in a loving if teasingly threatening manner.

"Well, brace yourself. I don't come out looking too good," Maggie admitted as she leaned against the counter.

Laurent took her in his arms and kissed her ear. "Do you really believe she stole the bracelet?"

"I can't imagine who else it could be."

"Without proof, *chérie*, you can only apologize and let it go."

"I know."

"And be thankful, eh? For the day? For dear friends? A warm bed to fall into tonight." He waggled his eyebrows playfully. "With me."

Maggie grinned.

"I am thankful. For all that. And for a man who sees me for who I am and loves me anyway."

He kissed her again. "Always, *chérie*."

"We could really use that gravy!" Windsor called and the table laughed. With Susie and Taylor gone, the tension and strain in the room had gone too.

They returned to the table and Maggie watched Laurent inspect the levels left in the dressing bowl and mashed potatoes before reseating himself, satisfied that there was enough for the next few minutes.

Windsor refilled his own wineglass and held the glass up, his eyes on Grace in what Maggie thought was a slightly drunken but definitely warm regard.

"For better or worse," he said and then made a face at his choice of words.

Maggie laughed.

"What we normally do about now," she said, "is go around the table and everyone gets a chance to say what they're grateful for in the last year or just in general."

"That sounds better than what I was going to say," Windsor said with an embarrassed grin.

Grace lifted her glass. "Shall I go first?"

Everyone nodded and she turned first to Laurent.

"I am grateful for you, dear Laurent, who literally gave me my livelihood and who had the faith in me that I didn't have in myself to pull my life back together." She glanced at Zouzou and her eyes were wet with emotion.

"I'm grateful for my daughter living in my home and making everything more wonderful every day. And for my dearest girlfriends, Danielle and Maggie." She lifted her glass to each of them. "And to you, Windsor. For trying as hard as I know you do. You're a good man and I'm grateful you're in my life."

"I'm going to cry," Windsor said, his eyes filling.

"Nonsense," Grace said, wiping her own eyes.

"This is a very lovely tradition," Danielle said to Maggie.

"I know," Maggie said. "It helps you remember what's important. Who's next?"

Mila raised her hand.

"Okay, Mila, you have the floor," Maggie said, gazing at her beautiful daughter and feeling her heart swell with pride.

Mila raised her water glass in a toast and looked straight ahead.

"I'm grateful for my friends," she said. "And my family. And the roof over my head." She swallowed hard.

Maggie frowned. Mila was not usually a terribly serious little girl.

"And I'm really, really sorry," she said in a whispered rush. "But I stole your bracelet, *Maman*."

THUMPETTY THUMP THUMP!

Maggie started coughing until Danielle was forced to pound on her back and Windsor shoved a glass of water in her hand. By that point, Laurent was on his feet and so was Mila.

Maggie saw Laurent had his hand on his small daughter's shoulder and was pointing her toward the hallway and his study.

"Did...did she say what I think she...?"

Jemmy's eyes widened. "Mila said she took the bracelet," he said. "And now she's really going to catch it!"

Maggie was on her feet, her napkin falling to the floor.

This couldn't be true! It didn't make sense!

Maggie hurried after Laurent and reached the door to his study just as he was closing it.

"You can stay but I will handle this," he said firmly.

Maggie agreed and he closed the door behind her. Mila had already gone to the leather chaise in the corner of Laurent's study. Mila loved to sit in this chair and would do so many evenings while Laurent worked on the vineyard business.

Today she sat on the edge of the seat as if it were made of razor blades, her head down, her hands in her lap.

"Speak," Laurent said to her gruffly.

"I wanted to wear it," Mila said, her head still down.

"Look at me," Laurent said and Mila looked up without moving her head. Her cheeks were already streaked with tears.

This just didn't make sense!

"Go on."

"It...it was pretty and I thought it would make me look grown up. I didn't think *Maman* would notice."

None of this made sense! Maggie's mind whirled. The jewelry box on its side was not how a little girl played dress-up. It was the setting of someone who'd been interrupted and needed to act hurriedly.

"Why confess now?" Laurent asked.

Mila shrugged and looked down again.

"Mila," her father intoned.

She looked back up at him. "I saw Taylor getting into trouble and everybody upset so I thought I'd better tell the truth."

"When did you take it?" Maggie asked, still not willing to believe it was Mila over Taylor.

"After breakfast. When everyone was busy outside with the dogs."

"My jewelry box was tipped over."

"I'm sorry, *Maman*. I heard someone in the hall and I jumped up but my sleeve got caught on the box lid."

Unfortunately that sounded like an honest recitation of what probably had happened.

Maggie felt a heaviness in her chest as she watched Mila in obvious shame and contrition.

"Where is the bracelet now?" Laurent asked.

"That's just it," Mila said, looking up in growing panic. "I put it in the baby's bed in Uncle Windsor's room but now it's gone."

It's been stolen twice?

Laurent leaned on the side of his desk, his arms crossed and observed Mila. Maggie wanted to scoop the poor heartbroken munchkin into her arms but she knew she couldn't. Mila had not only taken something she shouldn't have—she'd allowed someone else to take the blame.

"You will stay here in my study until I come for you," Laurent said.

Mila nodded miserably.

"No pumpkin pie for you. None of *Mamère's* apple tart."

A tear streaked down Mila's cheek and fell on her hands folded in her lap.

"Maggie?"

Maggie looked at her husband and saw he was indicating she should leave now.

He probably sees I'm seconds away from throwing my arms around her.

Torn between wanting to tell Mila not to worry but also wanting Laurent's punishment to stand firm, Maggie hesitated until she saw Laurent raise an eyebrow at her that warned her not to dispute him.

She reached out and touched Mila's arm and the child looked at her with hope and shame in her face.

"We'll see you in a little bit, sweetie," Maggie said.

Surely I don't need to tell her how disappointed I am, do I?

The look on Mila's face confirmed that indeed she did not.

Maggie left the room with Laurent behind her. He put a hand on the small of her back to gently prod her back to the dining table as if not completely sure she wouldn't turn around and liberate the little wrongdoer immediately.

And frankly she was tempted. Because the fact of the matter was, something just didn't feel right about Mila's confession.

∼

Maggie was surprised to see Susie and Taylor had returned to the table in their absence and were clearly making up for lost time by piling on turkey, dressing and candied sweet potatoes onto their plates.

For someone who doesn't like turkey, Susie surely is making a good show of enduring it.

Windsor didn't look at them when she and Laurent returned so Maggie knew he had probably run upstairs to tell his wife and daughter of Mila's confession.

Now Grace sat with the baby in her lap feeding him pieces of turkey dipped in Laurent's amazing gravy.

"I told you, didn't I?" Taylor said. "I told you I didn't do it."

"And Maggie already apologized to you for that," Grace said to Taylor. "And she did it *before* she knew it was Mila so you can quit braying."

"You see how she talks to her?" Susie said to Windsor. "*Braying*. Like a donkey. That's what she thinks of you, Taylor."

It was so clear that for whatever reason Susie was using Taylor to antagonize Grace.

Yet, just by watching how Susie and Taylor interacted with each other it was also clear to see there was no love lost between them.

Does Taylor *know* that Susie is just pretending to be on her side to goad her mother? Maggie wondered.

Very probably. But because it upsets Grace, Taylor is all for it.

What in the world happened there? Was Taylor always so hateful?

Maggie thought back to all the times in Taylor's childhood where she'd made everyone around her miserable, so filled with anger and hate and bitterness, that she couldn't stop long enough to feel the love her parents were giving her —until even they were at the end of their capacity to endure.

"I don't care what she thinks of me," Taylor said, finishing off the mashed potatoes. "I never did."

"You are very near the edge," Laurent said quietly and all heads swiveled to him and then back to Taylor. Maggie saw the silent warning that passed between them. He would have no show of disrespect at the table. And it didn't matter whether it was Thanksgiving Dinner or cheese and crackers in front of the TV. Not in his house.

"Sorry," Taylor mumbled.

Laurent and Danielle went to the kitchen to get the tart and the pumpkin pies and to bring the coffee in. Maggie got up to help but Danielle shooed her back to the table.

The last place Maggie wanted to be was at that dinner table.

She held her hands out to Zircon and the baby reached for her. Maggie took him from Grace and sat down with him, happy to have a distraction that didn't involve watching Taylor and Susie shovel food in their mouths when everyone else had already eaten. Zircon grabbed Maggie's hair with hands sticky with mashed potatoes and gravy.

"Oh, careful, Zircon!" Grace said, and reached for him.

"I don't mind," Maggie said, and kissed his face. "You're a treasure, aren't you, little man?"

"That's what she says now," Susie says, "until she finds him in her bedroom going through her jewelry."

"Be quiet, Susie," Windsor said, pouring himself another glass of wine.

"You think that won't happen someday?" Susie said.

"I think you need to be quiet."

Grace ran a hand lightly on Zircon's head and smiled fondly at him.

"Windsor and Susie have offered to let this little one come to live with me," she said.

For a moment Maggie didn't think she'd heard correctly. Her mouth fell open and she looked at Taylor but the girl was taking advantage of the fact that Laurent wasn't in the room and was reading her phone screen. Oblivious. Uncaring.

And then Maggie looked at Susie, so big and pregnant. Susie glared back at her. And it all made sense.

This had always been a trip with a reason. And the reason was to get rid of Taylor's baby. *Before* the new baby came. The *wanted* baby. Windsor and Susie's baby.

"Wow," Maggie said, kissing the baby's head. "This is big."

She looked at her friend. How in the world was Grace going to run a bed and breakfast and care for an eighteen-month old baby? She barely had the resources to keep things running as it was and Zouzou was able to take care of herself.

A baby would push Grace beyond her ability to run the business and stay sane.

Maggie glanced at Zouzou who seemed to be in a daze. And not a pleasant one.

"Wow," Maggie said again.

"Why do you keep saying that?" Susie said as she dribbled a line of gravy down the front of her velveteen jumper.

"I don't know," Maggie said. "I guess because it's sort of a big deal."

Laurent came out then with a tray of coffee cups and two French presses. The scent of the coffee swirled in the room around him.

"Jemmy," he said and immediately Jemmy jumped up and began grabbing dirty plates and stacking them.

"Quietly," Laurent said to him as he set the coffee down. "And help *Mamère* with the pie."

Jemmy carried the stack of dishes into the kitchen.

"Windsor wants Grace to take Zircon," Maggie said to Laurent.

He glanced at Maggie and then Windsor. "Is that right?"

"Seems like a better idea than where he is," Windsor said uncomfortably.

"It's because I'm probably going inside for a while," Taylor said around a mouthful of sweet potatoes. "Like that matters."

At first Maggie couldn't make sense of her words. And then she knew. *Inside.*

Taylor was going to prison.

Maggie looked at Windsor and he shrugged helplessly.

"I've done what I can. If the trial goes well, she won't need to but you know...her lawyer's not hopeful."

"My lawyer's an idiot," Taylor said.

"I'm sorry to hear that," Maggie said, not knowing what else to say.

"Oh, give me a break," Susie said. "Said the mother of the jewel thief."

Maggie flushed and refocused her anger on Susie,

knowing she shouldn't. The woman was just trying to antagonize her.

"First you spend all day accusing Taylor of a crime we find out *your* kid committed," Susie said. "That must gall you to have it be little Miss Perfect Angel. I hope you learned something from today."

Fortunately, Maggie glanced at Laurent and resisted the urge to walk over to Susie and dump the crystal bowl of cranberry sauce over her head. Laurent's expression was serene but definite: *They'll be gone soon. Let's finish this without assault charges.*

Maggie dearly wanted to ask who'd taken the bracelet that Mila said she'd put in the baby's bed but the look Laurent was giving her was clearly an edict to let it go.

At least for now.

At least until they got through Thanksgiving Day.

And that was going to take everything Maggie had.

LET IT SNOW, LET IT SNOW, LET IT SNOW

Pumpkin pie was never so interminable.
As Laurent cut wedges of pie and Calvados apple tart, the baby began to fuss so Grace and Zouzou went upstairs to put him down in his crib. Taylor helped herself to two large wedges of pumpkin pie at which point Maggie saw Laurent take his own advice and let it go.

As Susie forked into her third piece of pie swimming in so much whipped cream that Maggie had gratefully retreated to the kitchen to man the egg beaters in order to make more. Susie asked Laurent where Mila was.

"She will not join us for dessert," he said.

"I should think not," Susie said. "Unbelievable really. But then some parents are just so lenient with their kids that they can literally get away with grand larceny. Make no mistake, this is a parental problem. Although I saw something in her eyes when we first came—didn't I say so, Windsor?—I saw there was something shifty about that kid."

"Don't talk about my sister like that!" Jemmy said hotly.

"Jemmy, leave the table," Laurent said.

Jemmy glowered at Susie and then looked at his father. He gestured to his uneaten pie. "Can I bring...?"

Laurent nodded and Jemmy gathered up his plate, shooting Susie one last murderous look and went to sit in front of the TV in the next room.

Grace and Zouzou came down stairs from the baby's room.

"So since the mystery is solved, where is the bracelet?" Susie said around a mouthful of too much pie as Maggie brought another bowl of whipped cream to the table.

"Mila put it in the baby's bed," Laurent said sipping his coffee, his eyes on Taylor. "But it's not there now."

"So it's been taken a second time?" Susie said, a dollop of whipped cream quivering on her bottom lip.

"Apparently."

Taylor pushed away from the table.

"Where can I smoke?"

Laurent nodded at the French doors that led to the garden and Taylor went outside letting the dogs out as she went.

"Is that okay?" Windsor asked Laurent. "Will the dogs run off?"

"Let us join them," Laurent said, standing up. "The fresh air will do us good after such a heavy meal."

"That sounds lovely," Danielle said, standing up. "I think I'll join you."

With only the sounds of Susie's energetic chewing and slurping to interrupt the quiet of the table, Laurent, Danielle and Windsor fetched their coats and left the room. Maggie reached out and gave Grace's hand a squeeze.

Maggie wondered if Laurent had checked on Mila while she was whipping the cream. Mila's punishment was starting to feel excessive to her. She looked in the direction of Laurent's study and its closed door.

Susie finally pushed her plate away. "Ugh. Too sweet."

Is that why you ate three pieces? Maggie thought.

"It's freezing down here." Susie looked around.

Maggie guessed she was looking for Windsor to fetch her a sweater from upstairs, before she remembered he wasn't available.

And if she thought for a minute that anyone else at the table would go get it for her, she hadn't been fully present for the last hour to accurately gauge the animosity level of the room.

With obvious and noisy annoyance that she was being put out by her husband's thoughtless absence, Susie got laboriously to her feet and lumbered over to the stairs leaving only Grace and Maggie at the table. Zouzou stood up with her plate to bring it to the kitchen when Maggie stopped her.

"Zouzou, would you mind checking on Mila?"

"Sure, Aunt Maggie. Only Uncle Laurent already had Jemmy bring her a piece of apple tart."

"Oh, he did?" Maggie should have known there was no way Laurent could tow such a hard line with his little princess. "Okay. Never mind then. Thanks."

"He told her she could come out if she wanted but I think she's too embarrassed."

Zouzou took her plate to the kitchen and then went to join Jemmy in the living room to watch TV.

The French door jerked opened letting in a blast of frigid evening air and Taylor came in rubbing her arms from the cold outside. She hadn't grabbed a jacket before she'd gone out. She came back to the table and poured herself a cup of coffee.

"You got anything I can put in it?" she asked.

"There's cream and sugar on the table," Grace said.

"No shit."

"Watch your language," Grace said.

"I meant like whiskey," Taylor said.

"I'm afraid you'll need to endure this year's Thanksgiving as sober as the rest of us," Grace said.

But Taylor reached across the table and took her father's still-full wine glass and drank it down. She set the glass down and looked belligerently at her mother.

"You're too old for me to scold," Grace said softly. "You make your own choices."

"Like going to prison, Mother?" Taylor said sarcastically.

"For one. And having a child you never wanted."

Grace was Catholic and Maggie knew she'd been very unhappy over Taylor's refusal to find an adoptive solution for Zircon. It would have meant giving the baby a loving home—not the mishmash of anger and resentment he'd been born into.

"You were the worst mother ever," Taylor said.

It was the right button to push as Taylor of course knew.

Maggie felt a flair of defensive ire. Grace was very sensitive about the kind of mother she'd been and while she hadn't been perfect—*are any of us?*—she had loved her girls and tried her best. The last couple of years had been hard ones as Grace fought to accept at least some responsibility for the person Taylor had become.

"I know, darling," Grace said wearily as she excused herself to visit the downstairs bathroom. Maggie had noticed Jemmy was in there and told Grace she'd stand better luck going upstairs to the one at the end of the hallway. Grace turned toward the stairs.

"Does it really help saying that kind of thing to your mother?" Maggie asked Taylor when Grace had gone.

"What do you care?"

Maggie realized then that Taylor was incapable of believing that anyone did care. After all these years and after everything that everyone had done for her to show her otherwise, she just couldn't wrap her head around the concept enough to accept it.

"I was wrong to think of you first as the one who stole the bracelet," Maggie said.

"Yeah, you were."

"I hope things work out for you, Taylor."

Taylor snorted and reached for what was left in the bottle of red wine by Windsor's place. She drank what was left in it straight from the bottle and set it down hard.

"Whatever," she said with an insolent smile.

Suddenly, Maggie was aware of raised voices coming from upstairs. She turned to look in the direction of the stairs just as the French doors opened and Windsor, Danielle and Laurent returned with the two dogs bounding in front of them.

"Don't you dare, you bitch! I'll see you hurt for this!" Susie screamed.

Obviously Grace had run into Susie upstairs and tensions had escalated. Maggie stood and faced the stairs.

"Is everything okay?" she called and then waited until she saw Grace hurrying down the stairs, a look of triumph on her face and her hand outstretched with something in it.

"You are never going to guess who I found trying to hide a gold bracelet in the folds of your bed duvet cover!" Grace said.

LAUGHING ALL THE WAY

The gold bracelet twinkled in Grace's hand where she stood under the rustic chandelier in the dining room.

Maggie looked at Grace who had an expression of grim satisfaction on her face. Susie was thumping heavily down the stairs, her heavy breathing evident from twenty yards away.

"Susie was trying to plant the bracelet in our bed?" Maggie said as Laurent and Windsor joined her where she stood at the table.

"No!" Susie said, as she reached them, her breath now a series of labored wheezes. "That's what Grace wants you to think!"

Windsor turned to his wife.

"Are you saying *Grace* was planting the bracelet?" he asked.

Susie paused. Maggie could see by the woman's expression that she was either hesitating because she was unsure whether she could sustain such a lie or because she hadn't thought of it herself.

Grace didn't let things get that far.

"No, Windsor," Grace said. "I was passing in the hallway when I saw Susie in Maggie and Laurent's bedroom leaning over their bed. When I entered the room, she turned with a guilty look on her face and there on the bed I saw where she'd just dropped the bracelet."

"Oh, Susie," Windsor said unhappily.

"I can't believe you're going to believe her over me!" Susie wailed.

"So that's not what happened?" Windsor asked, looking from his wife to his ex-wife.

Susie sputtered and looked at the bracelet and then at Taylor at the table.

"Well, that's not the whole story!" she said finally.

"Oh, Susie," Windsor said again, dejectedly, and turned to Maggie. "I am so sorry, Maggie."

"Would you listen to my side of it?" Susie said. "This bitch—"

"Don't call her that," Laurent said and Maggie tried to remember the last time she's heard such cold warning in his voice. She got an image of him throwing Susie's suitcase into the back of the rental car before he escorted her out right behind it.

The image must have come to Susie's mind too because she blushed darkly.

"I was just trying to make things right," she said before glancing at Taylor.

A motion out of the corner of her eye made Maggie turn to see that Mila was standing in the open door of Laurent's study, listening.

"Oh my God," Taylor said standing up dramatically and knocking over the empty bottle of wine in the process as she addressed Susie. "You total hypocrite! You *did* think it was me who stole the bracelet!"

"Taylor, no!" Susie said. "I found it in the baby's bed this afternoon and I just wanted to put it back somewhere where—"

"She found the bracelet in Zircon's bed," Taylor said, her words slurring now. "And thought I'd taken it so *she* took it and waited for an opportunity to return it so you'd think it hadn't been stolen after all."

For somebody who's well on her way to being totally stinking drunk that's a pretty accurate summation of what probably happened.

"I was just trying to help!" Susie said to Taylor.

"Except that before Mila confessed you thought *I* was guilty!" Taylor shouted. "You're no better than my mom!"

"Enough," Laurent said to Taylor. "Go upstairs or go back out to the garden."

Taylor visibly fought to control her indignation and then turned on her heel toward the stairs.

"I was just trying to be helpful," Susie wailed as Taylor passed her. She reached out for the girl but Taylor jerked her arm away to avoid contact with her.

"Nobody ever believes me!" Taylor said from the stairs. "I hate you all!"

She turned and ran up the stairs.

Maggie turned to look at Laurent who was shaking his head.

Windsor ushered Susie into the living room and Danielle went to fetch her a glass of water while Grace sat back down at the table with Maggie. Laurent shooed Jemmy and

Zouzou from the living room, instructing them and Mila to start on the dishes in the kitchen.

Grace turned to Maggie. "Can you believe any of this?"

"Families," Maggie said with a shrug.

"I guess so. Listen, darling, I never thought I'd say these words in this house but does Laurent have any more wine?"

As if he'd read her mind, Laurent appeared with a bottle of his own label from a few seasons past. Danielle joined them at the table.

"It is still better than a body in the cellar," Laurent said philosophically as he filled everyone's glass.

"Not funny, Laurent," Grace said, fighting back tears as she reached for her wine.

Laurent reached over and squeezed her hand.

"You know we will help with the baby," he said.

"I know." She took a long sip of wine. "I know."

"You will of course change his name," Laurent said, a smile tugging at his lips.

Grace laughed, her tears chased away. "I was thinking maybe Phillip," she said.

Laurent nodded. "*Phillipe* is good."

Grace turned to Maggie. "I'm just so sorry. So so sorry."

"Don't be ridiculous," Maggie said. "What in the heck did *you* do?"

Windsor came into the dining room and sat down. "Is there any more pie?"

"Of course," Laurent said. "For you or Susie?"

"Susie. I'll take whatever you're pouring. Maggie, I am so sorry about all this."

"Stop apologizing, please. I feel bad enough. If I hadn't gone rooting around Taylor's room none of this would have happened." She glanced over at Danielle who gave her a wan smile.

The sounds from the kitchen served as a soft background as Laurent poured Windsor a giant balloon of the Domaine St-Buvard red. Windsor took it and a large slice of pie back into the living room.

"I should've known this would happen," Grace said, sipping her wine. "Or if not this then something like it. I must have been out of my mind to ask you to invite them."

"Why did you ask?" Maggie asked. "I mean with all the tensions and unresolved issues, was it just because you missed Taylor or wanted to reconnect with her?"

"No, that wasn't it," Grace said and glanced involuntarily toward the noises coming from the kitchen. "I'd given up on that."

Suddenly it was crystal clear why Grace had wanted them to come. An idea came to Maggie and she turned to Laurent.

"What is the extent of the punishment you've devised for Mila?"

"I told her she may have no friends over except Zouzou until after the holidays."

Maggie stood up. "Can you please keep Jemmy out of the kitchen for a few minutes?"

Laurent narrowed his eyes at her but nodded.

"Jemmy," he called. "Come with me to check the shutters by the front door."

Jemmy appeared in the doorway drying his hands, his eyes bright at the thought of any chore with his dad that might involve climbing a step ladder.

Maggie turned to Grace and Danielle. "Thanksgiving is almost over," she said. "Don't feel you have to stay on my account. It's been a hell of a day. I understand completely."

Grace and Danielle looked at each other.

"In that case we may go on home then in a few minutes,"

Danielle said. "Once you're finished talking with Zouzou." She arched an eyebrow and Maggie wondered, not for the first time, how Danielle was able to see things so much sooner than anyone else.

Maggie went into the kitchen. Zouzou was at the sink up to her elbows in suds while Mila stood solemnly next to her and ready to dry.

"Zouzou, your mom and *Mamère* are going to want to head out in a few minutes," Maggie said.

Zouzou and Mila shared a brief covert glance.

"I should finish the pots first at least," Zouzou said.

"Mila can finish them. Right, Mila?"

Mila nodded and Maggie leaned against the kitchen counter.

"Boy, people are really upset in there," Maggie said. "Your stepmother is trying to set a world pie eating record and Taylor is probably ripping the studs out of the walls in your bedroom, Mila. Plus you know, Zouzou, that your father is totally driven to distraction."

Maggie let the silence sink in.

"But of course that was the goal, wasn't it?" Maggie said.

It hadn't taken much rumination for Maggie to figure out that there was still one piece of the mystery left—in fact the most important piece.

And she wanted to give Zouzou every opportunity to tell her about it on her own.

Zouzou looked at Mila who gave her an angry look in return.

"Mila didn't tell me," Maggie said. "But I wonder if she mentioned to you that she's not allowed to have any friends over until January?"

Zouzou stared at her feet. Her lip quivered.

"Is that a yes?"

Zouzou nodded, her head hanging.

"Kind of a severe consequence, don't you think? when all she did was do a favor for a friend?"

Maggie watched the agony on Zouzou's face and she reminded herself of the impetus that must have driven the girl. She'd been very tempted not to say anything at all. But in the end Mila had done a favor for her friend and was ready to take the punishment for her.

At the very least Zouzou needed the opportunity to step forward and show she was worthy of that friendship.

"It was me, Aunt Maggie," Zouzou said. "I asked Mila to take the bracelet."

"Why?"

Zouzou worked hard to hold back the tears that were threatening. Her voice cracked when she spoke.

"To make Taylor look bad."

"Why?"

"I don't know." She continued to stare at her shoes, refusing to look up. "I guess because my dad loves her best and she's horrible."

"Surely you know that after all the trouble Taylor has caused over the years, if her dad was going to like her best—and I'm not saying he does—her stealing the crown jewels wouldn't matter."

The first tear slid down Zouzou's cheek. "I knew that."

Yet you did it anyway.

Maggie's heart went out to Zouzou. To know that stealing the bracelet would likely make no difference but still asking Mila to do it anyway showed just how desperately discouraged Zouzou must be. As happy as she appeared outwardly, baking, living at the bed and breakfast with Grace and Danielle, there were still issues of the past that continued to wound—and maybe always would.

Maggie turned to Mila.

"Did you think stealing the bracelet and lying about it was any less wrong because it wasn't your idea?"

"No."

"Especially since the point was to get someone else in trouble?"

"No, *Maman*. And besides, it got me in trouble instead," Mila said with a faint smile as if, miraculously, she was able to appreciate the irony of that.

"I'm still one hundred percent disappointed in you, Mila."

"I know." Mila's face fell and Maggie knew the child was thinking of the very important someone else who was disappointed in her too.

It was all well and good to take responsibility for your actions but when you're used to being Daddy's adored little girl, making such a major misstep hurts.

"You know what I think?" Maggie said to Zouzou, "I think you need to apologize to your sister."

"Taylor hates me."

"I don't think that's true but even if it were, it's not the point. You wronged her. You intended to frame her for a crime you hoped everyone would think she committed. Do I need to tell you that's wrong?"

"No, Aunt Maggie. Please don't tell Uncle Laurent."

Why does everyone care so much what Laurent thinks? Maggie thought in amused frustration.

"And then you need to tell your parents."

Zouzou looked stricken.

"Don't worry. You're too old to spank."

Somehow that didn't seem to reassure Zouzou.

FAITHFUL FRIENDS WHO ARE DEAR TO US

That night Zouzou made her confession to both Windsor and Grace and apologized to Taylor through her closed bedroom door before going home with Grace and Danielle, her head hanging in disgrace. Windsor had looked totally bewildered as to why Zouzou had had Mila steal the bracelet.

But Maggie could see that Susie was only too eager to fill in the gaps for him. And not in a way that would benefit anyone.

The next morning was a quiet one. Laurent was doing the finishing touches on tidying his kitchen—as if it wasn't already spotless—and pulling out dishes and containers from which he'd create his usual culinary magic for lunch. The scent of coffee and bacon still wafted delicately in the air in testimony to breakfast fifteen minutes earlier.

Mila and Jemmy were watching cartoons in the living room with their pancakes and mugs of cocoa while Maggie sat at the counter over a steaming coffee cup and tried to process this her fourteenth Thanksgiving in France.

Windsor, Susie and Taylor were in the garden. Taylor

was smoking and Maggie watched as she threw her still lighted cigarette butt at the dogs who, although they were in no real danger of being hit, nonetheless kept their distance from the girl.

Susie was bundled up deep into her coat, looking like a roly-poly Winston Churchill with steam coming from her lips as she spoke to Windsor who listened obediently with his head down.

Maggie turned away from the sight of the three of them to address Laurent.

"I need you to run interference for Zouzou," she said.

"And I need you not to interfere with that family," Laurent responded.

"Laurent, please. If you don't frame what Zouzou did for Windsor in a way he can understand he's going to get it all wrong. *Zouzou wants his love and attention.* She's not like Taylor. She's not bad for the pleasure of being bad."

"I know that."

"I don't think Windsor does. He's not imaginative. He sees what Zouzou did as Taylor 2.0. Please, Laurent. Talk to him."

Laurent glanced through the French doors to see Susie literally hanging on Windsor's arm and talking loudly to him.

"Zouzou needs someone on her team," Maggie said.

"It won't do any good," Laurent said. "Windsor has all he can handle right now."

He gave her a look that Maggie translated without needing him to say it out loud: the unspoken problem that everyone knew but poor Zouzou.

The fact that Zouzou was not Windsor's biological child.

Grace had always worried that that might someday serve

as an impasse to Windsor being able to connect and love Zouzou.

Maggie now saw that Grace had good reason to worry.

"I know it must be hard to put aside the hurt and betrayal you'd feel," Maggie said, "if you knew your child was really fathered by your wife's lover."

Laurent snorted. "Not in France," he said.

"Well, Americans aren't as evolved," she said. "And Windsor is even less evolved than most. Zouzou loves him, Laurent."

He nodded. "I will talk to him."

That morning, after a brisk walk around the vineyard with Laurent, Windsor organized an impromptu shopping trip to Aix for Taylor and Susie. When he dropped his wife and daughter off in Aix, he handed his credit card over to them and then drove with the baby to Grace's bed and breakfast where he handed Zircon to Grace and picked up Zouzou.

He told Grace not to wait up for them. He and Zouzou would spend the day walking the Cours Mirabeau in Aix and visiting Cezanne's studio which Zouzou had not seen yet. They would have dinner in one of the cozy brasseries in Aix and then later, he would bring Zouzou to Domaine St-Buvard where Grace could pick her up the next day.

Since he was driving to Marseille early the next morning for their flight home, Windsor said goodbye to Grace and promised he would stay in better touch with both her and Zouzou.

Grace would later tell Maggie that Windsor then kissed little *Phillipe* goodbye and drove away with Zouzou.

That day the Dernier family had their home to themselves again—at least for a little bit. They spent it picking at leftovers and watching reruns of American gridiron, playing with the dogs in the garden and talking on the phone to family and loved ones back in the States.

Maggie wasn't exactly sure what Laurent had said to Windsor nor was she confident it would last. But she did know that having her father all to herself for a day was probably more than Zouzou could have dared hoped for in her wildest dreams.

And it only took a ruined Thanksgiving and everyone accusing everyone else of grand theft to make it happen, Maggie thought with a smile.

That evening before Windsor and his crew returned and after a mouthwatering supper of oxtail macaroni gratin and garlic soup, Laurent and Maggie sat on the couch with Jemmy and Mila and the two dogs, Buddy and Izzy, in front of a roaring fire with "*The Wizard of Oz*" on the television.

Laurent—as he did every year—pretended not to understand why the movie was considered a Thanksgiving movie classic in north America and why, if one watched it even once, there was ever a need to watch it again.

"Hey, I don't give you a hard time about Jerry Lewis, do I?" Maggie said nudging him in the ribs with her elbow.

"You are confusing me with someone many generations older than I," Laurent said as he wrapped an arm around her and kissed her ear. "I will always prefer Van Dam."

"I rest my case."

Mila looked up at her parents. "Is everything going to be okay with Zouzou?"

"Of course," Laurent said.

Mila glanced at Maggie who smiled reassuringly at her.

Indeed. If her papa says so, how can she doubt it?

Mila turned back to the yellow brick road—happy and secure in her own cozy little world of love and security.

And that's when it occurred to Maggie that this moment right now, sitting in front of the TV set and fireplace, full of food and wine, and the absolute security that they would always be there for each other, was the very essence of Thanksgiving.

Regardless of the spilt gravy, the screaming fits at the table, the accusations and tears—the fact that her children could relax in the comforting traditions of a certain annual movie, an expected feast with all the familiar flavors they'd had since babyhood, combined with the comfort and assurance that they were loved and would be loved no matter what—that's what really mattered.

Could there be a better message to give or receive on this day? Maggie thought as she looked at her husband.

Laurent leaned over and kissed her.

"One of our better Thanksgivings, *non*?" he said with a smile.

Maggie felt a laugh bubble up inside her that made her feel warm all the way to her toes.

"I was just thinking the very same thing," she said.

<<<<>>>>

If you've just discovered Maggie Newberry and have a penchant for France and mysteries, you might want to see how it all began. There are currently thirteen books in the popular Maggie Newberry Mysteries and more added every year.

The Maggie Newberry Mysteries

Murder in the South of France
Murder à la Carte
Murder in Provence
Murder in Paris
Murder in Aix
Murder in Nice
Murder in the Latin Quarter
Murder in the Abbey
Murder in the Bistro
Murder in Cannes
Murder in Grenoble
Murder in the Vineyard
Murder in Arles
The Maggie Newberry Mysteries: Books 1,2,3
A Provençal Christmas: A Short Story

LAURENT'S THANKSGIVING DRESSING

You will need:
2 lbs. pork sausage
3 medium onions
3 16-oz packages of bread crumbs
2 cups chopped celery stalks
¼ cup minced fresh sage leave
¼ cup minced fresh thyme leaves
½ TBs fresh ground black pepper
1 to 2 cups chopped walnuts or pecans
2 eggs
6-8 cups chicken broth

Preheat oven to 350 degrees
Cut celery into 1/4 inch pieces and parboil.
Dice onions to make 3 cups and set aside.
Remove sausage from casing and sauté in large Dutch oven. Drain off grease.
Add diced onions to sausage and cook over medium heat until onions are soft.
Mix in celery, sage, thyme, and walnuts or pecans.

Add stuffing mix.

Add chicken broth—enough to make very moist—and stir until homogeneous.

Whisk eggs in a small bowl and fold into sausage mixture with a wooden spoon.

Let mixture set for 10 minutes.

Bake uncovered for one hour.

A Thanksgiving in Provence. A Maggie Newberry Holiday Novella. Copyright © 2018 by Susan Kiernan-Lewis. All rights reserved.

MAKING SPIRITS BRIGHT

I never really thought of myself as someone who enjoys Christmas. Growing up, Christmas was always a nonevent. My mom was never into it—she didn't cook and we didn't live near family—and then there was the fact that my father was never around. I can't say I felt like I'd missed out. Not really. I mean I always enjoyed dressing up for the odd office Christmas party but none of the festive hoopla ever really meant much to me personally.

I was thinking these warm and fuzzy thoughts as I hurried back from the village of Chabanel on a frozen, snowy afternoon a week before Christmas where my militant roommates, ninety plus year old twin sisters, had coerced me into going to pick up an ingredient for the dinner they were making that they insisted was needed absolutely *immediatement*!

It had snowed last night so riding my bike to town was out of the question. As it turned out, that was a good thing since as I made the last turn out of Chabanel down the country road that led to *La Fleurette*, the ancient stone *mas* where I lived with the twins, I soon discovered that I'd need both hands free.

There is a creek that fronts the small forest running from Chabanel to *La Fleurette* and beyond. While I never thought the creek needed it, there was a small stone footbridge that led to a path through the woods to Lake Robert beyond.

I held the bag of lemons I'd gone to town for in one hand and shielded my eyes with the other from the glaring sunlight bouncing off the snowdrifts beside the road.

There on the footbridge knelt a man, shabbily dressed and thin—someone I hadn't seen before around the village and trust me I've seen everyone.

One thing I've learned about living in a village—even on its outskirts as I do—is that it is perfectly acceptable, in fact nearly mandatory, to view with suspicion any strange person who happens to cross your path.

And this guy was *strange*. Not just strange-to-me strange but *weird* strange. He was kneeling on the bridge tying his shoe—or so it appeared—so as I walked by I had plenty of time to scrutinize his clothes and his manner and hypothesize about what he might be up to—again, all generally applauded actions by any villager anywhere.

When he stood up, he turned and glared at me. He spat out a few ugly words in my direction. I will spare you the translation but they were along the lines of *piss off you nosey cow*.

But I wasn't going to piss off. Not a bit.

Not when I saw that the burlap bag on the ground by his feet was not only moving but *meowing*.

I approached him and pointed a finger indictingly at the burlap bag.

"Where you go with that?" I asked in my most imperious bad French.

He repeated his earlier salutation at me—the whole *piss off cow* thing—at which point I did something I have done once in the past with great effect. I pulled out my nonworking cellphone and barked into it: "Police! *Immediatement! Au secours!*"

And would you believe his eyes got round as he momentarily forgot that cellphones no longer worked, and he turned and bolted across the bridge and into the woods.

Leaving his mewing bag of just rescued contraband behind.

THE KIDS ARE JINGLE-BELLING

There were four kittens in the bag.
    As I sat on the cold ground with my arms full of mewing, pouncing adorableness, it was all I could do not to rage over what that bastard had intended to do.

There is a special place in hell for people who hurt animals.

I stood up with the kittens now back in the bag and headed back to Chabanel. Tempted as I was to return immediately to *La Fleurette*, I knew that presenting *les soeurs* with our new family members without at least trying to find homes for them was a great way to have them dig in their heels and for the kittens to end up in a different burlap bag and on a different footbridge.

So I fought the cold and my growing weariness and went back to the village where I spent the next hour sitting at Café Sucre and somehow managed to give away all except one before my *café crème* got cold.

I don't know what there is about Christmas and a kitty's hard luck tale—or maybe it was the fact that every villager in Chabanel was presently having a rampant mouse problem—but I was astonished to find homes for almost all of them in such a short time.

And honestly? A little disappointed too.

Not that I didn't have plenty of critters back at *La Fleurette*. I had two cats, a wonderful little dog and a good assortment of goats and chickens.

The kitten nobody wanted was black with four white socks. Unfortunately, there was something wrong with one of its feet. When I placed it on the table, it limped.

I'd never seen a cat limp before. I thought it was impossible for them to hurt themselves but this little fellow was definitely lame.

"Just like Tiny Tim," I said, tucking him into my coat and buttoning up so only his little nose and two blue eyes were visible. "Which is what I'll call you because you are now officially mine."

Happy with the success I'd had in re-homing Tim's brothers and sisters, confident I'd now receive no grief from *les soeurs* after said effort, and buzzing with the effects of my café crème, I walked home to *La Fleurette*.

The place was in full swing when I arrived.

And by that I mean the sisters had Christmas-ed the crap out of the place. Even from the road—and even without electric lights which we no longer had since the EMP walloped us and all of Europe last summer—the place was aglow with candles and kerosene lamp light that you could see from fifty yards away.

Which was good since the daylight was already fading by the time I finally made it up the front gravel drive.

La Fleurette is a twelfth-century carriage house on the

outskirts of Chabanel. It's mostly stone with a wide back terrace with acres of gardens and in the winter the inside is always freezing.

An elderly goat that did not belong to us was grazing in a small patch of grass it had uncovered from the snow. An old bicycle was propped up by one of the large anchoring lavender bushes in the front drive. I didn't recognize the bike but since it was here, that meant its owner was someone the sisters didn't hate.

I don't want to say the sisters are xenophobic because they aren't at all. They know everyone in town and have lived here for going on a hundred years. But by this time they have their own solidly entrenched opinions about everyone. If they didn't like you fifty years ago you don't stand much of a chance of them liking you today.

I used to fuss at them for this but they responded that they knew more than I did and when I was ninety-five years old and had lived through a world war then they would listen to me. But hey, I'm no dummy. Even I know they won't be around to win that argument when I'm ninety-five years old.

I went in through the front door and heard laughter coming from the kitchen—not unusual for our house. I shrugged out of my coat, keeping Tiny Tim close to my chest with one arm and carried the bag of lemons into *la cuisine*.

Gathered around the table was Jean-Pierre Beaubien—the village chestnut vender (can you even imagine saying such a thing in Valdosta or Little Rock?)—and his two little girls, Alys and Clotilde. *Les soeurs* had made hot chocolate and sugar *palmiers* and a luscious aroma of cinnamon, caramelized sugar and vanilla greeted me.

"Jules!" Justine Becque the elder of the elderly twins

called to me, and then her face froze when she saw what I was carrying.

"*Le petite chat!*" the little girls squealed and ran to me their hands reaching for Tim. Both of them were about six years old, and they were dressed in rags. And not mended, tidy rags either.

"Careful," I said to the girls. "His foot is hurt."

They made the appropriate cooing sounds and I carefully handed the kitten over. They sat and cuddled him on their laps.

"What is this?" Léa Cazaly, the slightly younger of the elderly twins, asked sharply.

"A Christmas miracle?" I said brightly. "Hello Monsieur Beaubien. *Joyeux Noël.*"

"*Joyeux Noël*, Mademoiselle Hooker," Jean-Pierre said with a broad smile. I thought he looked a little older than the forty years I'd been told he was but he was always so cheerful. The sisters said he was a flirt, but harmless and kind.

Jean-Pierre had no family left in the village but his people had been in Chabanel since before Charlemagne. And he was a widower. His wife had died of cancer five years ago.

Making a living selling nuts can't be easy. And unless you're able to somehow turn them into fuel (hint: you can't) it was probably even harder making a living selling them *after* the EMP.

Léa went over to the kitten and picked it up and narrowed her eyes.

There was nothing warm and solicitous about her manner. If I didn't know her better, I'd say she was about to toss him out the kitchen window.

She made a noise she often makes—kind of a cross

between a snort and a raspberry. Really lovely if you've never heard it before.

"*Entorse*," she said finally, handing the kitten back to one of the little girls. "Not broken."

Justine set out a dish of cream and Alys put Tiny Tim on the cracked tile floor where the little thing began to earnestly lap the cream until it was all gone.

"Someone was fixing to drown him," I said. "Some guy I'd never seen before had this one and three more—"

"Eh?" Léa looked at me with alarm and then turned to look behind me as if I were keeping the others hidden behind my back.

"Don't worry," I said. "I went to the village and pawned them off on Madame Basso, and also Marguerite and Mary-Ester Toureille. Happy?"

"*Pas du tout*," Léa snorted, nodding at Tiny Tim.

A hissing sound made me look in the direction of the window where my cat Neige was sitting, her eyes like yellow slits. I wasn't worried though. His hissing didn't mean anything. Neige didn't even like *me*.

"Everyone can just chill," I said. "Tiny Tim needs a home and we're it. Merry Christmas." I looked at Léa as if ready to do battle with her over this but she just shrugged and went back to warm up some cocoa for me.

Have I mentioned how nice it is to come home after rescuing the world's downtrodden to people who make cocoa for you?

Definitely starting to feel like Christmas.

THE OLD ONES NEAR FORGOTTEN

Madame Joslin tapped a spoon on her china saucer. The coffee was already cold but Bella was of course long gone back to the kitchen. If she rang for her, it would still take the stupid woman twenty minutes to answer.

Pathetique.

It was impossible to get good help. Worse of course here in Chabanel, she reminded herself sourly. Bella and her equally useless husband Stephan were not from Chabanel. Even if they had heard the rumors, they wouldn't care. It had all happened too long ago for them to care.

And my money spends too nicely for them to mind.

She stood up and walked to the window of the living room so that she could look out over the long expanse of lawn. It was covered with snow and the light had faded until only the long strangely threatening shadows of the trees displayed on the blank canvas of white lawn.

A form emerged from the forest who she recognized immediately as Stephan. He no longer carried the burlap bag so he had probably thrown *that* into the lake as well as the cats.

Idiot.

As Madame Joslin watched Stephan trudge up to the back of the house where he would join his wife in helping to make dinner, she found herself wondering if the kittens had felt anything as the cold water hit them before being mercifully dragged to the bottom.

She turned from the window.

Did it matter if they did?

As long as they were finally free?

AS WE DREAM BY THE FIRE

That night at dinner, Luc came over as he was now back in the habit of doing. In the six months since I'd known him, it was only recently that we'd officially started actually dating and so far, for whatever culturally obscure reason, this did not involve crawling into bed with each other.

Not that I was worried. Luc had made it plenty clear that he found me attractive and after all he was French! So, sooner or later I was pretty sure something was going to happen in that department.

After introducing Luc to Tiny Tim and embellishing just a tad the story of how I'd acquired him, we all settled down to a lovely meal of Coquilles Saint-Jacques that *les soeurs* had put together.

As the Chabanel chief of police, Luc knew everyone in town so I wasn't surprised to hear he knew the weird would-be cat killer I'd just described to him.

"Sounds like Stephan Guoin," he said, spooning up a hearty bowl of the rich seafood casserole

Both *les soeurs* sucked in their breath at once when he

said that which, granted wasn't that unusual—a butterfly flitting about the rosemary bush in late October could bring on the same reaction—but it made me realize that the guy wasn't a total stranger.

"Do you know him?" I asked them.

They did their usual bit of looking askance at each other and clucking and wagging their heads so that they answered me but didn't at all answer me.

So annoying.

Thank God for Luc.

"He and his wife are the servants of Madame Joslin," he said. "She lives in the *Dedans* at the edge of town."

Which explained why I hadn't seen him before. I honestly thought that property was abandoned.

"Do you think his employer knew he was out drowning kittens?" I asked.

Luc grinned. "I am afraid when it comes to France's overpopulation of cats, most country people are not as soft-hearted as you," he said. "If they have no need for a mouser, it is just another mouth to feed, especially now."

I glanced at *les soeurs*, expecting them to confirm this exceedingly hard-hearted view since they were the toughest old broads I had ever known. But strangely, they didn't seem to concur. Both studied their dinner plates as if they'd stopped listening. Something I knew for a fact was not the case.

"So do you know Madame Joslin?" I asked them.

"We do. *Malheuresement*," Léa said solemnly.

Before I could ask what the hell *that* meant, there was a vigorous pounding on the door which of course, being under ninety years old and the hostess, it was my job to answer.

On the threshold I found Eloise Basile—Luc's sergeant

—but before I could invite her in, Luc was behind me and already pulling on his coat.

"What is it, Eloise?" he asked.

"A reported theft and a sighting of the culprit," Eloise said. "Matteo is off tonight and you said always to go in tandem."

"*Oui, oui*," Luc said, hurriedly kissing me before slipping out the door. "Apologize to *les soeurs* for me!" he called before disappearing into the darkness.

GONE AWAY IS THE BLUEBIRD

"A stolen goose?" Luc said in frustration as he drove to town in the iconic 2CV they used as a police car—one of the only gas-powered vehicles in Chabanel.

"Not just any goose, Chief," Eloise said. "This one was thirty pounds." She looked at her notes. "Fattened in Nimes, delivered to Madame Joslin and butchered and hung in her outdoor shed early this morning."

"A goose," Luc said shaking his head.

Ever since the EMP had happened the caliber of crimes in the village had changed drastically. With money taking on much less importance, things like food, working flashlights and batteries had quickly ascended in value—making the theft of such things more serious.

"She reported that the goose was missing at seventeen hundred hours which also happened to be the time when Jean-Pierre Beaubien visited her house."

"The chestnut seller?"

"*Oui.*"

"So they think the chestnut seller stole their goose?"

"Madame Joslin's handy man or whatever he is, Stephan Guoin, reported seeing Jean-Pierre leaving the grounds with a very large bag—one easily big enough to carry a goose."

Was it odd that Guoin has been called to his attention for the second time in one day?

"I can't believe you interrupted my dinner for a stolen goose," he said.

"A goose would be valuable any time of year, Chief," Eloise said earnestly. "But especially at Christmas."

"*Oui, oui,*" Luc said tiredly as he drove to the *Pijou* neighborhood on the east side of Chabanel.

Like most homes in Chabanel, the *Pijou* where Jean-Pierre lived was dark and, Luc had no doubt, cold. Most villagers had figured out stoves for heat and cooking but the fuel was still expensive and hard to come by. The mayor's office helped where it could, but there were still many who were cold and hungry in the village.

Luc parked the car down the street and tapped the steering wheel with his fingers. Outside the stone façade were the chalk drawings of a child.

"He has children?" he asked, frowning.

Eloise looked at her notes. "*Oui.* Twin daughters. Six years old."

They got out of the car and walked to the front of the garage attached to Jean-Pierre's apartment. In a normal world, Luc would never have dreamed of searching the garage without a warrant.

But many things had happened since the EMP changed everyone's lives last summer. Now they did not bother with warrants.

"The lock is not engaged," Eloise noted.

Would you put stolen items in your garage and then not lock the door? Luc wondered as he pushed open the door.

Apparently so.

There on the table in full view was a very large plucked goose.

SLEIGH BELLS RING, ARE YOU LISTENING?

T he thing about living in a small village is that there is literally nothing that can happen without everyone knowing about it almost immediately.

That's because everyone is watching everyone all the time.

I honestly have no idea how people think they can have affairs or collect kinky porn or skip flossing and not have the entire village talking about it by dinnertime.

So it was no surprise that by the time *les soeurs* had once again forced me out of the house and back to the village the next day—this time to pick up sausages—I had already heard the news of how Luc had arrested Jean-Pierre for Grand Theft Goose after he left my house.

I should possibly mention here that the news one picks up from helpful but nosey villagers is not always Associated Press level reliable.

Before I even went to the *charcuterie* to pick up *les soeurs'* andouillette—and then over to the bakery for the almond croissant I had my heart set on—which should tell you how indignant I was over the arrest—I went to the *Police Municipale* to confront Luc.

The police receptionist, Madame Gavin, who sits at the front desk gave me an immediately sour look when she saw me walk through the door. I know she doesn't like me but she knew her boss was my probably-boyfriend and so she didn't go beyond just making a face.

Luc's second in command, Adrien Matteo, was another matter but wasn't hateful to me today for two reasons. First, things had gotten a bit better between us after he'd saved my life a few months back. And second, he wasn't in the office this morning.

Nodding imperiously at the receptionist, I went straight to Luc's office, knocked and let myself in. I could tell by the look on his face that he was surprised to see me barge right in but I've learned from experience that if you've got a bone to pick with someone, waiting politely on their threshold sends altogether the wrong message.

"Are you kidding me?" I said indignantly. "Scrooge much?"

I can assure you my words—rehearsed and well thought out on my stomp over to his office—were unfortunately totally lost on him.

Arghh! This language problem is such a pain!

"Jules?" he said with an expression with is the damnedest combination of a smile and a frown.

"You arrested Jean-Pierre?" I said. "Seriously? What part of *it's Christmas* don't you get?"

"So all criminals are to be forgiven at Christmas?" he said with a full-on smile now.

"He has two children! Where are they now? At Chabanel's Child Services? Oh wait. There isn't one."

I had him now. Luc was totally defenseless against my

superior moral argument and he knew it. I tapped my foot, ready for whatever feeble response he might attempt to throw at me with. Except one.

"I didn't arrest him."

"Eh?" I mentally re-ran the memory tapes of where I'd gotten my information. Monsieur and Madame Mischuk and then confirmed by old man DuPree over by the *charcuterie*.

Yep. Infallible news sources all of them.

Except they weren't.

"Jean-Pierre agreed to turn himself in after Christmas so that we might get to the bottom of this," Luc said reasonably. "He is accused of stealing a goose and that is not a small crime these days. But of course, as you say, it is Christmas so he is home with his family."

I blushed because there is seriously nothing worse than having the moral argument ripped out from under you by the person who got there first.

"Okay. Well all right then," I said in a restrained huff, attempting to regain some of my dignity. "And I assume we may expect you tonight for dinner?" I asked sternly.

"Of course."

"Good," I said, nodding curtly and backing out of his office while he continued to do that smiling-while-frowning thing he does.

My visits to the *charcuterie* and the *boulangerie* took me no time at all so that by the time I got back to *La Fleurette*, I was fully and completely back into the Christmas spirit which—if you recall—is a phrase I never expected to hear myself utter.

Once more I walked into the front door to the

welcoming fragrance of cookies baking. Cocoa was curled up in his favorite place in the world—in his down-filled dog bed on the kitchen floor so he could be in prime position for any possible food droppings.

The two cats, Camille and Neige had in the last twenty-four hours thoroughly inspected Tiny Tim and while neither of them gave any hints of wanting to become surrogate mothers to the poor thing, neither did they seem ready to chew his eyes out either. They were both sitting as close as was felinely possible to the stove without risking ruining the pleasant ambiance of the room by the smell of burnt fur.

I scooped up Tim and sat down in the kitchen while *les soeurs* rooted through the bag from the *charcuterie* and made their usual assorted noises of satisfaction—or not—that I'd become accustomed to in the last six months of our acquaintance.

"So," I asked, "did you hear the news that Jean-Pierre is being looked at as a person of interest in a stolen goose case? It's why Luc had to leave last night."

Both sisters looked at each other before speaking which made me realize, as usual, that they knew way more about it than I did.

"It was Madame Joslin's goose," Justine said. "Her man said he saw Jean-Pierre with the goose in his hands."

"And then it was found in Jean-Pierre's garage," Léa said.

"Really?" I said. *Did Jean-Pierre really steal the goose?* "That's not good."

"*Pas du tout*," Léa agreed as she hauled out the grinder and began unwrapping the sausage. I knew she knew that the butcher was perfectly capable of grinding the sausage for her to any degree she liked but I'd long given up reminding her of it.

"Why is it you two don't like Madame Joslin?" I asked

abruptly—often the only way to catch the old girls off guard enough to get a straight answer out of them.

"She is a traitor," Léa said simply.

"I'm assuming you mean during the war," I said. "So she's...elderly?"

"She is a few years younger than Léa and me," Justine said. "While we worked our part in the war, Madame Joslin and her husband were working for the Vichy."

I knew the Vichy was the French arm of the Nazi party. Members of Vichy were hated during the war, pitting neighbor against neighbor, and were brutally punished for their activities afterward.

"I see. So I'm guessing by the way you keep looking at each other that all came to a head in some way?"

"One of Madame Joslin's neighbors, Victor Campeau, came to the Resistance with evidence of Monsieur and Madame Joslin's activities. Monsieur was executed and—"

"Whoa! Wait. What?" My mouth hung open. "What do you mean *executed*?"

Léa shrugged. "He was hung."

"Jules," Justine admonished. "He worked for the *Germans*."

"And since of course his wife was well aware of his activities she was...humiliated," Lèa said with satisfaction.

I knew what that meant. *Humiliated* was the French euphuism for tarred and feathered. Ouch.

"And yet she still lives on in the village?" I asked, shaking my head in wonder.

"Oh, *non*, she left after the war," Léa said. "She moved to Lyons. She only came back to Chabanel three years ago."

"Why?"

"Why what?"

"Why did she come back?"

Both sisters frowned. "Because Chabanel is her home, of course," Léa said as if speaking to a verifiable idiot.

I let that sink in for a moment because it was a shock to me—a shock on the level of if they'd just told me that squirrels could take the SAT in France.

Why would you ever want to return to the place that murdered your husband, knew the terrible deeds you had done, and had put hot tar on your very probably naked body?

But in any event it did clear up *why* Stephan Gouin was working for Madame Joslin.

Obviously it was because he was the only one in the village who would.

CAROLING ALONE IN THE SNOW

It was now three days before Christmas and the village of Chabanel had officially begun to burst at the seams with unmitigated holiday madness. I don't know what the place would have looked like in years past with full-on electricity but without electricity it was still nothing less than magical.

Because it got dark so much earlier now, the shops in the town used candles in their windows to showcase their wares which made the whole village look—at a glance—like a Victorian Christmas card. Tinsel and evergreen garlands were strung from every store lintel, the statue of the French WWI soldier that stood in front of the *maire* now wore a fir wreath around his neck studded with holly, and there were flickering lamps lining the main walkway through the village.

You couldn't live anywhere in town and not realize that Christmas was definitely coming

Which was why it was so odd to be standing on the doorstop of Madame Joslin's mansion and realizing that it exuded about as much holiday cheer as a mausoleum in January.

That is to say, none.

I'd decided to talk to Madame Joslin face to face because while everything was skittles and beer right now vis-à-vis the stolen goose, Luc had stressed that the piper would need his sixpence as soon as Christmas was behind us and that meant the goose case would need to be investigated.

Ergo my visit to the owner of said goose.

I naturally assumed that Madame Joslin would be on the back foot with me or any visitor from Chabanel. After all she was the village pariah. She and her husband had betrayed the town. She knew the French even better than I did. There would be no forgive and forget from them. I don't care how many people got lynched or touched up with road tar.

Which is why I was so surprised when Madame Joslin not only answered the door herself but snarled at me with a decidedly unrepentant affect.

"Madame Joslin?" I said pleasantly.

"*Qui êtes-vous?*" she said coldly.

"My name is Jules Hooker," I said in a very friendly manner expecting her to be overcome with gratitude to have someone treat her kindly for a change.

Yeah, uh, no.

"*Allez-vous!*" she said, waving me off her doorstep like I was the neighbor's dog.

I decided to ignore her shocking response to my magnanimous munificence and plunged on with the point of my mission.

"I am here to ask you to relent in your accusation against Jean-Pierre Beaubien," I said. "Monsieur Beaubien has two children under the age of—"

"His two children did not prevent him from stealing my goose," she said tartly. "Why should they be a consideration in my forgiving the crime?"

"Well, there's some question as to whether or not Monsieur committed the crime."

"Which is why we have magistrates. He will get his day in court."

"I was hoping you could eliminate the need for that. I mean, it is Christmas after all."

"What do I do the rest of the year when Monsieur Beaubien finds a need to steal from me?"

"I don't really think—"

"I don't know who you are, Mademoiselle, but I am very disappointed that Monsieur Beaubien is not in jail. He has committed a crime against me and is going unpunished. Are you his whore?"

"I beg your pardon?"

"If Monsieur Beaubien sends you to me again to plead for him I will have you arrested as well. Now be gone!"

And with that she slammed the door in my face.

TAKE A CUP OF KINDNESS YET

Luc looked out the picture window onto the *Place de le Maire*. They'd already put the tree up in the square and were busily wiring it to hang the ornaments that the children were making in the Chabanel school. It wasn't a large tree this year. They'd lacked the usual trucks and electric chainsaws that they normally relied upon when cutting down the village Christmas tree.

He was humming as he thought of his evening ahead with Jules. Yes, they were taking things slow. Deliciously slow. He could tell Jules was impatient with the pace.

That was just as it should be, he thought with a smile.

A sudden rap on the door broke into his thoughts and he turned to see Eloise standing in the doorway with her coat on, and her purse on her shoulder, leaving for the day.

"Problem?" he said as he splashed on the after shave he kept in his desk drawer.

"Adrien came back to report that the witness corroborated the identity as Jean-Pierre Beaubien."

Luc felt a sudden brief onset of queasiness. "And?" he said.

"He left again immediately to question the suspect."

"The witness confirmed that he saw Monsieur Beaubien at the church?" Luc said wearily.

"Yes, Chief. Most definitely. Adrien said it was definitely confirmed that the church poor box had been full of clothes and money just this morning. And now it's gone. Do you want me to meet up with Adrien?"

Luc grabbed up his jacket and felt his blood pressure rising.

"*Non, non,*" he said. "You go on home. I'll go."

Merde, he thought as he pulled on his jacket and charged through the waiting room to the front door of the police station.

Why did he have a bad feeling about all this?

TALK OF LAST YEAR'S GLORIES

I think it was safe to say my visit with the notorious Madame Joslin had not gone well. For whatever reason she was determined to see Jean-Pierre held responsible for the theft of her goose—which made no sense! She was clearly rich. The bird was big enough to feed a fourth of the village! The whole thing just felt like spite.

As I made my way back to *La Fleurette*, I was anticipating an amazing dinner of *moules marinières* that I knew *les soeurs* were putting together—not to mention Luc's delicious company. Luc usually brought a bottle of wine with him—thoroughly delighting *les soeurs*—although he always joked that we were not to ask him where he got it.

Seriously. I'm not at all sure he's joking.

It hadn't snowed in two days so the snow on the ground had turned into muddy slush, the pristine whiteness of the winter picture postcard spoiled by the oily evidence of the few motorbikes that still worked, Luc's police car, and the multitude of farm animals that made their treks and therefore deposits up and down the roadway.

As I rounded the last bend in the road I saw Luc's police

car parked in the circular drive at *La Fleurette*. I felt a heaviness sift through my body. Luc normally walked to our *mas* so I knew this was just a quick visit to give his regrets.

What could be so important two days before Christmas that he needed to miss two dinners with me? I thought with annoyance.

I found him in the kitchen. He was standing—a bad sign—and the Madame Twins were doing their usual bustling dance of serving coffee and slicing great wedges of glistening chocolate éclairs for him.

"Hey, you," I said as I came in. Cocoa ran to me and after I finished tussling his ears, I turned to Luc. "You can't stay?"

He kissed me, a sad smile on his face. "*Je suis désolé,*" he said.

Which meant no, he couldn't stay.

"What is it this time?" But before he could answer me, I saw the answer to the tune of two very sad twin girls that I hadn't noticed sitting together in the window seat with Tiny Tim in one of their laps. There was an anticipatory tingling in my chest as I looked around for Jean-Pierre. I had a feeling I wouldn't find him.

"I had to arrest Monsieur Beaubien," Luc said. "The girls have no family in town so *les soeurs* say they may stay with you until arrangements can be made."

"What the hell, Luc," I said with frustration. "It's just a stupid goose! We'll pay for the damn thing!"

"It's not the goose anymore," Luc said, taking my arm and moving me out of the kitchen and away from the girls, even though I knew they didn't understand English.

"Monsieur Beaubien was seen moments after the church poor box was stolen."

"No way. Who saw him?"

"Jules, stop. I cannot tell you these things."

"I'll find out."

"No, you will not." Luc said, his nostrils flaring. "I heard that you visited Madame Joslin today and you will stop interfering. *Completement.* Do you understand me?"

So honestly I have to say it wasn't the best visit I'd ever had with Luc which pretty much ended with me turning on my heel and stomping upstairs like an annoyed teenager. After I heard his car leave, I came back downstairs.

Les soeurs had the two little girls at the kitchen table covered in flour and their little tear-stained faces absorbed in the task of making a *bûche de noel.*

Justine looked up when I came in and smiled sadly. I watched them for a few moments, commenting encouragingly to the little girls. I couldn't believe it was going to be Christmas in two days. Surely Luc wasn't going to keep Jean-Pierre in jail over Christmas?

When Léa went to the pantry next to the kitchen I followed her.

"I went to see Madame Joslin today," I said.

She turned to look at me and her face as usual showed no surprise.

"She doesn't seem a bit sorry about whatever it was she did in the war," I said. "At least that's my take. She threw me off her property!"

Lea rolled her eyes which I correctly interpreted as *that is no surprise.*

"Stay away from her. Madame Joslin and her husband got what they deserved. Now leave her alone."

The sounds from the kitchen came to us, muted and soft from the other room. The two little girls should have been laughing but I only heard Justine's soft and encouraging voice.

"What do you know about the church poor box theft?" I asked.

"Only what Chief DeBray has told us."

"Okay, so that's a crock," I said, knowing she wouldn't understand the word.

But obviously she did understand the intention. She narrowed her eyes at me.

"Does it have anything to do with Madame Joslin?" I asked. "Or her psychopath handy man?"

"I am not understanding you," she said as she pulled down a box of sugar from the shelf and turned to indicate that I was in her way.

"Why does Luc think Jean-Pierre did this?" I pressed.

She sighed and gave that time-honored Gallic shrug. "The witness this time was very reliable."

"Reliable? Who? Give me the name of one person in this village whose testimony is that unimpeachable."

"Father Bardot," she said.

THE BELFRIES OF ALL CHRISTENDOM

So what would *you* do if you knew that a man of God—the one who was about to be the ringleader to the year's big event—the person most known for mercy and forgiveness—held a man's life and the happiness of his children in his hands?

You'd go talk to him, right?

Which is why the first thing the next morning I bundled back up and went in search of Father Bardot at the Chabanel Catholic church.

The village church was situated—hidden really—in a stand of trees on the northern side of the main road that snaked through Chabanel. Its ancient gray-stone front blended into the dingy blue-gray of the landscape and its crumbling steeple presided over a small graveyard enclosed by a frail wrought-iron fence.

That's where I found Father Bardot. An old guy with heavy coke-bottle eyeglasses and a perennially red nose, he always seemed friendly but didn't speak a word of English.

As soon as I approached him, smiling and waving as I've learned that nearly all French love to be greeted by—I'm kidding—he put down the snow shovel he'd been pushing around like he'd been looking for an excuse to quit.

Before I had a chance to present my questions, Father Bardot began to speak to me in rapid French, the gist of which was that he hadn't seen me at Mass since I'd come to Chabanel. It occurred to me to say his eyesight was bad but I figured he might have other ways of knowing so I came clean.

"Me sorry me no be to church," I said contritely. "Me happy for Christmas!"

He winced because man of God or not he was also a Frenchman and I'm sure it hurt to hear me mangling his language.

But there were bigger fish to *flambé* here.

"You see Monsieur Beaubien steal the...poor box?" I said, waving in the direction of the church.

He looked surprised. But my big gift of the day came when he hesitated to answer me.

He wasn't sure.

"You *no* saw Monsieur Beaubien steal?" I said, fighting down my excitement.

"*Je ne sais pas,*" he admitted. Then he reeled off a bunch of French again way too fast in which I was only able to catch the name *Monsieur Gouin* and the fact that he seemed very regretful.

He was apologizing for something.

Like saying he saw something when he wasn't sure he did? I wondered.

"You were with Stephan Guoin?" I asked innocently.

He nodded.

"Did Monsieur Guoin say *he* saw Monsieur Beaubien?"

"*Oui.*"

"Okay. So maybe you....you *not* see Monsieur Beaubien?"

"*Non, non,*" he said vigorously shaking his head. It seemed he definitely *did* see Jean-Pierre that day but whether or not he saw him near the poor box or walking off with its contents—that was the part he now was not sure of.

I'll just bet Stephan Guoin put it in your head that you saw something you didn't.

As I walked away I felt a definite adrenaline rush. I was sure I'd just deep-sixed the prosecution's only reliable witness. So, unless they actually found the goods hidden in Jean-Pierre's apartment or something, I was well on my way to proving he had nothing to do with the crime.

With his happy thought in mind, I headed straight for the *Police Municipale* to lay my case before Luc and personally watch him release Jean-Pierre from jail. Moving down the hill toward the city hall near where the police station was, I thought a celebratory almond croissant was in order so I made a slight detour to the *boulangerie.*

The village bakery is pretty much my favorite place in the village even when it's not Christmas but during Christmas it is ramped up to a whole other level of awesomeness. Madame Fournier, the baker and proprietor, had clearly been baking into the wee hours because the range and amount of yeasty goodies far outstripped her usual inventory. She even had toile netting and red and green silk bows affixed to each glass shelf in her display window.

When it came my turn to order, Madame Fournier greeted me pleasantly enough and then mentioned that someone told her they'd seen me out to visit the Nazi-lover in the *Dedans.*

Surprised that she was so openly hostile about Madame Joslin, I nodded that it was true but did not respond verbally. There was only one almond croissant left and six people were behind me. Getting thrown out of line over a perceived insult would not work to my advantage if I wanted that croissant.

"Do you know Madame Joslin?" a woman standing in line behind me asked.

"I do not," I said, keeping my face as bland as possible. "An almond croissant, *s'il vous plait*, Madame Fournier."

"I suppose she will be happy now," Madame Fournier said as she bagged up the line croissant and handed it to me.

"Oh," I asked innocently as I snatched the bag from her. "Why is that?"

"Because Monsieur Beaubien is in jail, that is why!"

"Why would that make her happy?" I asked as I allowed the woman behind me to edge me out of her way.

"Because of course Monsieur Beaubien is the descendant of the neighbor who gave Madame's name to the Resistance seventy years ago!"

HEARTS WILL BE RACING

Jean-Pierre's family was the neighbor who tipped off the French Resistance about Madame Joslin and her husband?

It all made such complete sense now.

Madame Joslin tried to get Jean-Pierre arrested for stealing her goose. When that didn't work, she set up her man to rob the church and then make the old priest think he saw Jean-Pierre do it.

And it worked, too. Jean-Pierre was in jail.

And all because Madame Joslin had come back to Chabanel to get revenge on the people who'd killed her husband and ruined her life.

As I walked blindly in the direction of the *Police Municipale*, my thoughts in a whirl, I saw Eloise Basile coming my way—obviously heading to the *boulangerie*. She smiled and waved and I stopped.

"*Bonjour*, Jules," she said affably as we double cheek kissed.

"*Bonjour*, Eloise. What if I found out that the witness

who said he saw Monsieur Beaubien steal from the church box now says he didn't see him?"

Eloise glanced at the *boulangerie* over my shoulder as if realizing it was going to be a while before she got there and possessed whatever taste-tempting treat she'd been lusting after all morning.

"Is that what we will discover?" she said, narrowing her eyes at me. "That the witness we have will now recant?"

"Yep."

"Does Chief DeBray know this?"

"I'm just on my way to tell him."

"*Bon*," she said, starting to move away from me. "And what about the church box contents found in Monsieur Beaubien's bicycle basket?"

"Eh?" I said, feeling my stomach bottom out in a most unpleasant way.

"Talk to the Chief, Jules," Eloise said merrily. "I'm sure he will want to hear what you have discovered."

Crap. They found the church box contents in Jean-Pierre's bike basket?

I hesitated in the street. Going to Luc's now would only earn me another lecture about not interfering. If he'd found the stolen goods at Jean-Pierre's that probably trumped whatever any witness did or didn't see.

I shivered as a sudden chilly wind whistled down the narrow cobblestone street and seemed to push me along a different path.

I needed Madame Joslin to confess that she was deliberately planting evidence against Jean-Pierre.

It was the only way to prove that the circumstantial proof did not in fact lead to an admission of Jean-Pierre's guilt!

Satisfied with my new direction, I hurriedly gobbled

down my croissant, spilling a shower of buttery croissant flakes down the front of my bright red quilted puffer vest, and headed back to Madame Joslin's *mas*.

By the time I got to Madame Joslin's house, I was cold and I was hungry again. But I was also convinced that this was the right approach to take. There was no doubt in my mind that Madame Joslin and her henchman Stephan were behind the frame job on poor Jean-Pierre. A part of me thought that Luc, once he was presented with the facts of Jean-Pierre's relationship to Madame Joslin, would agree with me. But I've been wrong in that department before and I couldn't risk letting Luc know what I was up to in case *he* tried to interfere with *my* investigation.

Like last time, I rapped on the front door and waited. But unlike last time, nobody answered my knock. It had been a long walk from the village and while I hadn't been expecting a cookie and a cup of tea when I got here, neither had I expected my trip to be a total waste of time.

I wouldn't allow it to be a total waste of time.

I tried the doorknob and the door pushed open. That's not too surprising for the country. Most people don't lock their doors except at night.

My pulse was racing as I stepped into the foyer.

"*Allo?*" I called. "*Bonjour?* Madame Joslin?"

I waited in the hallway as the dust motes danced lazily in the air in front of the big picture window in the parlor. And then I closed the front door behind me and entered the house.

Like a lot of houses in the countryside in this part of rural France, I've noticed that sometimes the owners make an effort to create a front room that's knockdown gorgeous

—decked out with Italian luxury furniture and plush carpeting from Morocco—but if you tiptoe past it into the rest of the house you're likely as not to be looking at bare rock walls and prison style cots.

I don't know what the rest of Madame Joslin's house looked like but if I had to guess I'd say it was probably just like her front parlor—sumptuous and tastefully decorated.

Clearly, whatever had happened to Madame Joslin in the intervening years in Lyons had been good ones for her. She was rich. That was the first thing I noticed as I tiptoed around the living room. The second thing I noticed was that there wasn't a single item of Christmas ornamentation anywhere. She wasn't Jewish so it seemed odd not to have even a couple of Christmas cards out.

Thinking of correspondence, I moved to her desk in the corner of the room. Nobody had computers anymore and Madame Joslin was too old to have had one anyway. I saw a stack of mail on the desk and quickly sorted through them, my heart pounding in my throat.

I knew this woman would not hesitate to have me arrested if I got caught.

Or worse.

After all, she did once work for the Gestapo.

As I hurriedly sorted through her mail I felt a sudden hypersensitivity to my surroundings. What looked like a government envelope with a recent postmark caught my curiosity. I picked it up at the same moment I heard a door shut very close by.

Stashing the envelope in my coat pocket, I turned in time to see Stephan come down the hall toward me.

He saw me only seconds after I saw him. I looked at the front door, cursing the fact that I'd closed it.

And ran for it.

THERE'LL BE MUCH MISTLETOEING

I made it down the steps and halfway across the lawn before I realized the big lug was no longer chasing me. He was heavier than me of course but he was also older. And while I'm the first one to admit that being mean tends to make you faster than the average person, in this case it was no match for our age difference.

When I reached the trees at the end of the lawn, I turned and saw Stephan standing on the front threshold of the house watching me but not following. I'd had too much of a head start on him, I thought as I turned and made my way into the woods.

Unfortunately, I was pretty sure he'd be able to describe quite accurately a woman about my size and age wearing a tomato-red quilted vest.

Crap. If I didn't get a handle on my fashion proclivities I was never going to be any good at clandestine detective work.

***

By the time I got back to La Fleurette, the little girls were laying out their paper maché ornaments that we would then carry to the village square and put on the tree.

Any other set of circumstances would have found Alys and Clotilde giggly with delight but of course, today they worked woodenly, their little ruddy faces looking to be on the verge of constant tears.

Damn that Madame Joslin! She was single-handedly ruining Christmas for these kids—and very likely the rest of their lives too if she had her way.

I'd spent enough time with *les soeurs* to know the power of a grudge. But honestly the French bring it to a whole new level.

As I sat in the kitchen with the little girls while they very solemnly folded and boxed the little Mary and Joseph figurines and the sparkling gold and red balls they'd made with food dye and glitter, Cocoa came and put his chin on my knee.

Justine was overseeing the little girls and Léa set a cup of hot chocolate in front of me. I knew she wanted me to look at her so she could give me her wordless mind voodoo which is basically her reprimanding me for wherever it was I'd been all morning. But I wouldn't play ball by looking at her.

"*Merci*, Léa," I said sweetly as I pulled the stolen envelope from my pocket. It was a single page and I soon realized the second page of a letter. I read it quickly several times. I was right about it being some kind of government correspondence and while I wished I had the first page to get the full picture, I could tell it was a formal request for Madame Joslin to reconsider their proposition to her.

Without the first page, it didn't make sense but the romantic part of me began to formulate a theory that the government, thinking she'd suffered enough, was perhaps offering her a sort of formal forgiveness for war crimes committed.

As soon as I put the letter back away there was a knock on the door. Again, my job.

I hopped up and made my way to the front door which I opened to the sight of Luc standing there, looking extremely unhappy.

Bloody hell. Now what?

"*Bonjour* Jules," he said sadly. "Is this by any chance your goat?"

Past his shoulder I saw the old grey goat that belonged to the little Beaubien sisters.

It lay unmoving on the ground.

Trust me when I say that when things are not going well, you can pretty much count on a dead goat not improving the mood.

The little girls burst into tears at the sight of the animal and had to be forcibly removed so that Luc could drag the carcass out of sight until my friend Thibault showed up later to dispose of it.

I have no idea why the goat died—beyond old age—but I have to say he couldn't have picked a worse time.

Once *les soeurs* had removed the little girls back to the kitchen and plied them with sugar and cocoa—the time-honored remedy for anything from dead goats to murder charges—Luc steered me to the back terrace.

I should have known this wasn't a social call. For one

thing, it was in the middle of the day and for another, he didn't have a bottle of wine in his hands.

Hey, I'm a detective, remember?

I could also detect that he was annoyed.

I shivered in my thin wool sweater and looked longingly at the inside of the *mas*.

Was it possible my little escapade at Madame Joslin's had been reported? I was all set to deny the crap out of that when Luc pulled out a folded sheet of paper.

"A complaint against you," he said, his eyes flashing with annoyance.

"Is this because we haven't brought our milk bottles in at night? Because I told that nosy milkman—"

"I am glad you find this so amusing," Luc said, looking not at all glad.

"Luc, look. I assume this is Madame Joslin?"

"Are you saying there might be *another* complaint sworn out on you *besides* Madame Joslin's?"

"Don't try to distract me from the point," I said, hoping desperately to attempt to distract him from the point. "Isn't it true that you no longer have a witness to the church poor box theft?"

Luc hesitated. "Another witness has stepped forward," he said.

I rolled my eyes. "Let me guess. Is it Stephan Guoin? This is getting kind of monotonous, isn't it?"

"My thoughts exactly," Luc said dryly. "Back to my point, please. Were you or were you not at Madame Joslin's house today?"

"What if I was?"

"Then you will suffer the full brunt of my fury for once again ignoring my orders."

"I was there."

He ran a hand over his face and groaned. "Why you are doing this to me?"

"I'm not doing this to you! I'm trying to prove that Jean-Pierre is being railroaded!"

"I am not knowing this word."

"Madame Joslin wants revenge on Jean-Pierre because it was *his* family who alerted the Resistance to her husband's activities during the war."

"You have got to be kidding."

"Are you saying you don't think people's memories in Chabanel are that long? Half the time the old guys sitting around the Café Sucre are talking about World War Two!"

"And what makes you think Jean-Pierre is any relation to that neighbor?"

That stopped me. I tried to remember who'd told me that. I was pretty sure I'd gotten the information from somebody in line at the bakery. And I'd taken it as gospel. I probably should have verified it before going out to talk with Madame Joslin.

"I heard he was," I hedged.

"From whom?"

"What difference does it make? Can't we just go forward and confirm it? If he is related, then *bingo*! you have motive for Madame Joslin framing him. If he isn't then..."

"Yes, Jules? If he isn't?"

"I don't know," I said in frustration. "But I'm not willing to give up on this until the facts are confirmed."

"An unusual position for you, is it not?"

"Go ahead, take your best shot. I'll admit I should have confirmed it first."

"You mean before you went running off to Madame Joslin's?"

"Yes. Happy now? You were right. I shouldn't have gone off without knowing the facts."

"This truly is a remarkable day."

"My tolerance for your gloating is not limitless," I said primly. "And I would have thought it beneath you anyway."

He pulled me into his arms and kissed me.

"Do not be giving me ideas of putting you beneath me," he murmured into my ear, and effectively reducing me to the gelatinous substance that *les soeurs* sometimes create in the bottom of a sugar pan.

I was having trouble catching my breath and only Justine's entrance onto the terrace and Luc's subsequent release of me enabled me to begin breathing in regular spates again.

I cleared my throat and tried to remember what we'd been talking about before things got so deliciously derailed.

"So as I understand it," I said, smiling at Justine as she clipped a few leaves from the *potager* and retreated back inside, "you no longer have a witness claiming to have seen Jean-Pierre and the church box. Is that right?"

"As I said," Luc said with a grin, clearly enjoying my discomfort, "Stephan Guoin has come forward to offer his own eye witness testimony to the crime."

"But it's his word against Jean-Pierre's."

"The church box contents were found in Jean-Pierre's possession."

"Yes, because they were planted!"

"You don't know that," Luc said firmly. "And meanwhile I forbid you to approach Madame Joslin again. You are hearing me?"

"Of course, Luc."

He gave me a suspicious look and I gave him my very best *trust-me* look.

I didn't feel a bit bad about fibbing to him, because of course I had to go back and talk to Madame Joslin!

Any fool could see that.

TO FACE UNAFRAID THE PLANS THAT WE MADE

Maybe the third time is the charm? I asked myself as I knocked on Madame Joslin's front door imagining all manner of receptions from a shot gun blast to a spittle-flinging tirade from the Nazi-loving Madame Joslin to no answer at all.

I'm not sure which of three was least desirable.

Well, the shot gun blast of course, but you get my drift.

I was desperate for answers and this time I was not leaving without them.

It was the maid or the cook who answered the door. She was wearing an apron over a plain black dress. I'd been told that the cook was Stephan's wife. She was a mousey little thing with thinning brown hair and bad skin. Boy if anybody wanted to make a case for how all French women were beautiful or had an ingrained sense of style, they really ought to meet Bella Gouin, I thought and then chided myself for my ungenerosity. Married to Stephan—a man easily twenty years her senior—I decided I could cut her some slack.

"I am here to see Madame Joslin," I said pleasantly. "She me expecting," I added.

Bella grimaced as if answering the doors was a new chore to her roster of duties and not one of her favorites. She made a move to step out of the way which I assumed was her version of *please enter, Madame*, and a small brown object fell out of her apron pocket. Hurriedly she snatched it up and I entered the house.

"*Qui est-il?*" Madame Joslin's voice called from the other room. But Bella had already picked up her duster and wandered away from the foyer, leaving me to make my own way to the woman who'd already thrown me out once and sworn out an official police complaint against me.

So. Here was me not expecting a big welcome.

"*Bonjour*, Madame Joslin," I said cheerily, moving into the room.

True to form, Madame gasped and while she didn't jump to her feet, she did stiffen and look about her as if in search of a gun or some other weapon.

I'd discovered from my previous visit with her that her English was pretty good—probably from whatever work she'd done in Lyons—and so I switched to speaking English since I was not going to make a very good argument in French nor was I going to endear myself to her by my attempts.

"I am so sorry to be bothering you again, Madame," I said hurriedly. "And I promise if you talk to me I will leave you alone and never bother you again."

"Or I could just have you arrested and achieve the same effect."

I licked my lips and glanced around the room hoping the place wasn't bugged and not sure how it could be with no electricity. "Except I'm dating the Chief of Police," I said, "so I'm pretty sure I'm not going to be arrested unless I kill someone and even then…" I shrugged and held out my hands as if to say, *probably not even then.*

She snorted and crossed her arms. I haven't had much opportunity to enjoy my passion for beautiful clothes since the EMP had flung me and everyone else in France functionally back to the seventeenth century but I could definitely still appreciate fine fashion. Madame Joslin was wearing a tartan plaid dress with a flare hem that was just inspired.

"I love your dress," I said, wondering if it zipped in the back or buttoned. The older designers really knew how to work with fabric. "YSL, isn't it? Vintage?"

"Say what you have to say and get out."

"Sure. Okay. Now don't take this the wrong way but I was wondering if you knew that Jean-Pierre Beaubien happened to be related on his mother's side to…" I hesitated because now that I was getting down to it, I wasn't totally sure I could say the words.

It is amazing what people who lived through that war—right here where it happened—had endured. Living with *les soeurs* had taught me that.

The effects of the war had changed both the twins' lives forever, from Justine never marrying, and Léa never having children to both of them never trusting anything good in the world. So to accuse Madame Joslin of what I was about to—when it was probably her bedrock pathology—was actually not only dangerous on a whole bunch of levels, it was cruel.

"Yes?" Madame Joslin said impatiently. "He is related on his mother's side?"

There was something in her face—something defiant and unrepentant—that told me *she didn't know.*

And if she didn't know that Jean-Pierre was related to

the neighbors who'd sold her out, then there went my whole case because why else would she frame him?

"I...he is related to the Campeaus," I said softly. I had moved to face her on the couch and my back was to the correspondence desk where I'd found the envelope yesterday. Before I turned around, I saw the first page of the letter.

Madame Joslin was staring at me unblinking. I held my breath and I swear she must have been holding hers too because there was not a single sound in that room as she stared at me.

Finally, she spoke. "What are you saying to me?"

"I'm...I'm saying..." And by now I was not at all confident that what I thought was happening was actually happening.

"I'm saying that you had your man Stephan frame Jean-Pierre Beaubien because of what Jean-Pierre's people did to you in the war."

Her mouth fell open. And when it did I felt my knees weaken. You didn't need a lie detector test to see that she had no idea what I was talking about.

All I'd succeeded in doing was reminding her that nobody had forgotten about her disgrace of seventy years ago.

And that was so not what I wanted to do.

Madame Joslin's face blanched and she raised a hand holding a large school bell. She rang the bell and then dropped it onto the couch.

Within seconds, Bella appeared in the doorway.

"*Oui, Madame?*"

"*Je veux de l'eau,*" Madame Joslin said weakly. "*Vite.*"

I felt a thickness in my throat. I'd upset her. And I hadn't helped Jean-Pierre

Madame Joslin put a hand to her face to cover her eyes

and I realized she would not speak at least until Bella got back with the glass of water she'd asked for.

Should I apologize? Just slip out? Both seemed wrong. Instead, I turned to look out the window and saw Stephan shoveling snow from the walkway out front. As I looked back inside, my eyes fell onto government letter again and without thinking, I picked it up.

Madame was still sitting quietly on the couch, her hand across her eyes.

I glanced at the first page of the letter. The French was basic and easy to understand but even so I had to read it three times to confirm that I was reading what I thought I was reading.

The French government wanted to induct Madame Corrine Joslin into the National Order of the Legion of Honor for the undercover work she and her husband had performed during the war.

Something about the forged documents they'd created had allowed hundreds of downed pilots and Jewish children to escape Nazi-occupied France.

A sudden coldness hit me in my solar plexus at the realization of what I was reading.

Madame Joslin wasn't a traitor.

She was a hero! A hero who'd been punished by an ignorant, unknowing rabble her whole life.

I looked at Madame and saw that she was watching me sadly.

"Why didn't you tell anyone?" I asked, waving the letter. "They should know the truth!"

Bella came into the room with a glass of water and handed it to her mistress. She gave me an untrusting look and put her hand in her apron pocket.

The same pocket where she'd put the object after it had fallen on the floor. The object that I now was able to able to identify as a flattened, dark brown nut.

A chestnut.

The next thoughts came at me like an out of control locomotive.

Bella was the cook for this household.

She would go to the market to get produce. Jean-Pierre worked at the market.

Jean-Pierre was a flirt. He and Bella were the same age.

The realization hit me like a two-ton truck.

Could it really be that simple?

LAUGHING ALL THE WAY

I ran to the doorway and blocked Bella's exit route. The look on her face told me I'd guessed right.

"*You* stole Madame's goose," I said.

"*C'est ne pas ma faute!*" Bella said, looking worriedly at her employer.

"Yes, it is too your fault," I said. "You and Jean-Pierre were lovers."

"*Non, non!*" Bella said.

By now Madame Joslin had picked up the thread of things.

"Bella knows Jean-Pierre," I said to Madame Joslin, knowing there was no way I could interrogate Bella with my bad French. "Ask her if that had anything to do with her trying to pin a goose theft on him—and don't forget the poor box!"

Madame turned to Bella who, after a few sharp words from Madame—largely incomprehensible to me—collapsed onto the couch in tears.

It appeared that yes, Bella and Jean-Pierre had had a dalliance. He'd broken it off a few days ago and she'd been so angry that she told her husband that Jean-Pierre had tried to cheat her at the market.

It had been Stephan's idea to steal the poor box money and plant it on Jean-Pierre's bike and to then say he'd witnessed the crime.

By the time Bella's tearful confession was finished, she wasn't the only one who needed to sit down and have a drink.

As the tearful cook pleaded with Madame to forgive her I sank into a nearby blue silk Antoinette accent chair, the letter from the French government still in my hand.

I shook my head in wonderment.

Neither of the goose theft or the church poor box were connected to Madame Joslin or Jean-Pierre's family or the war at all.

GOD BLESS US EVERY ONE!

The next day was a whirlwind one of last minute preparations. After all, tomorrow was Christmas Day. After my triumph at Madame Joslin's and the subsequent release of Jean-Pierre from the Chabanel jail, the sisters had let me sleep in until nearly ten.

When you consider the amount of work they still had to do—and how much of that was going to be allocated to me—you'll understand what a gift that was.

We were so busy getting the cakes and roasted meats and their accompanying sauces in order, packing up the buckwheat crêpes and *magret de canard* that the day flew by. Just before six in the evening, my good friend Thibault came by with his Citroen 2CV and we carefully packed the baked goods, the garlands, the ornaments, the meats, and ourselves into the back seat.

What with the hour growing quickly later and the fact that Madame Joslin and the Guoins were the ones the Chief of Chabanel police had needed to spend most of his time with, I'd only seen Luc briefly yesterday. I knew he was happy to be able to free Jean-Pierre whose two little girls were beyond delighted to see their papa again. They'd all spent last night with us but were gone before I awoke.

Thibault had been out of town for a few days visiting family outside Paris but he'd wanted to be back in Chabanel for Christmas.

I knew some of Paris had electricity back on but I felt sure that even Paris couldn't compare with the magical Christmas fantasy that Chabanel had transformed into.

Thibault drove us to within a few cobblestone streets of the main square in front of the *maire*. A large Christmas tree had been erected next to the WWI soldier and it was festooned with strings and strings of battery-operated lights. The children were busy hanging their homemade ornaments.

Tables lined the square and were already groaning with baked goods, roasted meats and various alcoholic drinks. By what you saw tonight you would not know that this village was poor one. Or that it had any problem at all with feeding its denizens.

I even saw oranges. In December.

I knew the black markets in the surrounding area had done a fierce business in the weeks leading up to this day.

I picked Luc out of the crowd immediately although it looked as if he was on duty tonight. I was so ready to hear his praise for how I'd solved the two crimes—after of course he got through fussing at me for going to Madame Joslin's house when I'd sworn to him I wouldn't.

I also saw my nemesis Lieutenant Matteo in full uniform —as of course he would be—standing sternly next to a row of folding chairs with some of the older villagers already seated. Next to him sat Madame Joslin.

With a look of pure terror on her face.

This was troubling to me since I knew the woman was

probably an introvert at the least and a dedicated agoraphobe at the worst. Why was she here so clearly against her will? Was it so the village could publicly reproach her for not having better control of her hired help?

Neither of the Gouins were in attendance and I imagined that was Luc's doing. I heard he refused to incarcerate them over Christmas but I'm pretty sure he'd warned them off attending tonight's festivities. At least I hoped so.

I saw Jean-Pierre with Alys and Clotilde at the *patisserie* table. The goodies on display today were for enjoying, not buying, and already I could see chocolate on Clotilde's cheek.

"Mademoiselle Hooker!" Alys called out when she spotted me, my arms full of a large basket of glazed tarts. *Les soeurs* walked behind me equally loaded down.

I grinned at Alys and noticed several people turned to look at me as the sisters and I made our way to a bare table and began spreading out our baked goods. After that no fewer than half the village came over to hug and kiss me, and wish me and the sisters a *Joyeux Noël*.

It was like nothing I'd ever experienced or felt before. You know that part in the Grinch's story where his heart grows twenty times its size in about five seconds?

Yeah. Like that.

Our mayor Lola Beaufait, wearing a gorgeous lush Valentino dress in green velvet, was standing on the platform in front of the tree. I have often had issues with this woman but nobody can fault her clothes. Even in a post-apocalyptic village scenario, the woman has world-rocking style.

"*Joyeux Noël , tout le monde!*" she said to all of us. The crowd responded with shouts back of "*Joyeux Noël!*"

You are not going to believe me when I tell you that I

didn't have the time or the mental energy to remember to tell *les soeurs* about Madame Joslin's big secret. So when the mayor stood up and called everyone's attention to the fact that their own Corrine Joslin would be receiving the nation's highest medal of honor in recognition for her and her husband's work creating forgery travel passes during the war—work that cost her husband his life—and had enabled fifteen hundred downed Allied pilots and orphaned Jewish children to make it out of France safely, the sisters turned to me with a look of having been totally betrayed.

You knew and didn't tell us?

The mayor public apologized to Madame Joslin and offered a nation's and a village's undying gratitude for her and her husband's work during the war.

You know how I said the twins never changed their mind about people? Well, clearly the rest of Chabanel didn't subscribe to the same pathology. When I looked over to find Madame Joslin, she was literally swamped with people hugging and kissing her.

Even Matteo was no match for it.

After that—or rather during all this because the lovefest raining down on Madame Joslin didn't quit—the mayor turned on the battery-powered lights on the tree and the square was filled with the sounds of over two hundred people oohing and ahhing as only the French can.

I think I'm going to have to say that tree was the most beautiful thing I've ever seen. But that could be due to the prism of tears filling my eyes.

I turned to Justine and hugged her, and then Léa—although she was clearly still annoyed with me for not helping her be the first person in Chabanel to know about Madame Joslin's heroism.

I saw Jean-Pierre coming over with the girls with that

how can I ever thank you look on his face that I'm getting accustomed to seeing on people whom I've just helped spring from jail, but more importantly, behind him I saw Luc, standing there, looking at me and grinning.

And you know? I'm thinking that grin of his—so sexy and so proud of me all at once—was maybe the best gift of all.

Later that evening after we'd all drunk too much and eaten too much, but before the band was ready to give up playing music and everyone headed for midnight mass, I began to pack up what was left of the feast so that Thibault could put them in his car.

I saw Justine and Léa talking to Madame Joslin after some of the crowd had thinned and I knew they were inviting her over for Christmas lunch tomorrow proving that Christmas miracles do happen after all.

Jean-Pierre was with them, holding one sleeping twin in his arms. The other—Clotilde I think—stood beside Madame Joslin, and I was surprised to see that the little girl and Madame Joslin were holding hands.

Madame Joslin was a wealthy, lonely old woman, I thought. And Jean-Pierre and the twins are an instant family. I felt a warm flush of satisfaction at the thought that the four of them might find their way to each other.

Tonight is just one Christmas miracle after another.

I felt Luc's presence before I saw him, as he came up behind me and put his hand on my hips through my heavy wool coat. It was cold especially the later it got and everybody's breaths was showing up in vaporous clouds.

"So you have been busy," he said as I turned to face him.

I wasn't sure whether he meant tonight or the solving of two crimes or bringing a despised woman back into the village fold. As usual with Luc, his words typically had many different meanings.

"Am I in trouble?" I asked playfully, my heart pounding.

"I will have to think about that," he said, leaning in for a kiss. "How is your first Chabanel *Noël*?"

"If I told you it was my best Christmas ever, would you believe me?"

He arched an eyebrow at me and his eyes twinkled. "*Vraiment*?" he said.

As we stood there in each other's arms, the music playing and the sounds of people laughing and talking all around us, it began to snow.

My heart felt so full at that moment that I literally couldn't speak.

It was all too good, and too much.

So yes, Luc, *vraiment*.

This was absolutely and completely…

…the best Christmas ever.

A French Country Christmas. Copyright © 2017 by Susan Kiernan-Lewis. All rights reserved.

ABOUT THE AUTHOR

Susan Kiernan-Lewis is the author of the bestselling *Maggie Newberry Mysteries*, the post-apocalyptic thriller series *The Irish End Games, The Mia Kazmaroff Mysteries,* and *The Stranded in Provence Mysteries.*

To see sneak previews and giveaways as they happen, be sure and go my website at susankiernanlewis.com.

Books by Susan Kiernan-Lewis

The Maggie Newberry Mysteries
Murder in the South of France
Murder à la Carte
Murder in Provence
Murder in Paris
Murder in Aix
Murder in Nice
Murder in the Latin Quarter
Murder in the Abbey
Murder in the Bistro

Murder in Cannes
Murder in Grenoble
Murder in the Vineyard
Murder in Arles
A Provençal Christmas: A Short Story
A Thanksgiving in Provence

The Stranded in Provence Mysteries
Parlez-Vous Murder?
Crime and Croissants
Accent on Murder
A Bad Éclair Day
Croak, Monsieur!
Death du Jour
Murder Très Gauche
Wined and Died
A French Country Christmas

The Irish End Games
Free Falling
Going Gone
Heading Home
Blind Sided
Rising Tides
Cold Comfort
Never Never
Wit's End
Dead On
White Out
Black Out

The Mia Kazmaroff Mysteries
Reckless

Shameless
Breathless
Heartless
Clueless
Ruthless

Ella Out of Time
Swept Away
Carried Away
Stolen Away

The French Women's Diet

Made in the USA
Middletown, DE
30 November 2018